MW01133613

JOIN THE FAMILY

Want free stuff? Join my my Palms Family!

After you've read this book, I hope you'll check out my **Join the Family** page at its conclusion. There you'll find a special URL you can use to join my Palms Mommas and Palms Daddies. Use it to get free ebooks, bonus content, and updates about new releases.

The Maltese Jordans is coming soon!

THIS
A JACK PALMS NOVEL
IS LIFE

SETH HARWOOD

CRIMEWAV Books

Copyright © 2011 by Seth Harwood
All right reserved

No part of this book may be reproduced, or stored in a retrieval system, or transmitted in any form or by any means, electronic, mechanical, photocopying, recording, or otherwise, without express written permission of the publisher.

The characters and events in this book are fictitious. Any resemblance to actual persons living or dead is purely coincidental.

ISBN-10: 1717894631
ISBN-13: 978-1717894632

for my father

THIS

A JACK PALMS NOVEL

IS LIFE

"It's a cold world and this is life."

Part I

Beside the Law

1

As Jack sits up to steal a look over the back of the couch, he wonders if the person in his backyard is the one who set his bed on fire, burned it down to the frame. A welcome-home message from an unknown friend.

He can still see the remains in his mind's eye: the wood frame scorched black and the mattress crispy where the sheets and blankets used to be. Even Victoria's Tempur-Pedic pillows—the plastic foam you wouldn't think would be flammable—burned. A black line of charred rug outlined where the bed had stood, but nothing else in the room had been touched by fire. A professional pyro.

That was one of two disturbing items Jack found when he got home from the open road.

Another creak in the night, a stick breaking outside the patio doors. The VCR clock flashes 12:00; the wall clock reads two forty-five.

When Jack looks over the back of the couch, he sees darkness all the way to the rock wall of the garden. Then he hears another sound like the last but louder: a crunch from something heavier than a deer—someone walking outside, just past the little evergreen trees Victoria planted along the back wall of the house.

Jack hits the floor on all fours, crawls between the couch and the coffee table, then around the end table toward the double patio doors. Whatever's out there, he wants to know it before it knows him.

At first, all he sees is his own reflection in the glass. Then, just inside the edge of the garden, a glint of something metal pointing out of a bush—the shiny round barrel of a gun. Jack drops to his chest as the gun goes off. He hears the whistle of a silencer, and a bullet pierces the glass above him, right where he'd be if he had been standing.

He looks out through the bottom row of windows in the door, and sees a man come out of the bushes—a man right outside his living room, not five feet away. His face is hard to make out in the shadows, but he's white, serious-looking. Jack's seen him before, but that's just a hunch—maybe not even right.

The man in the yard raises the gun and its long silencer, and shoots three times through the right-side windows of the door. What he's shooting at, Jack has no idea, probably his own reflection. Shards of glass fall onto Jack's back, and he covers his head with his hands, hoping he won't hear another shot.

After a moment, he looks up and sees the three sets of metal locks at the top, the handle, and the bottom of the door, and goes to slide the first one. To his surprise, it's already open. He tries to remember if he locked it, but he hasn't thought about doing that since he left for his road trip with the Czechs. Or maybe his bed-burner left it unlocked.

He gathers himself into a four-point stance, his arms straight down from his shoulders, hands on the floor, and his legs bent behind him, resting on the balls of his feet.

He focuses on the shooter's knees, hoping the man is still looking at his own reflection. The shooter steps forward, oblivious to the crunching sound from the wood chips in the yard. And that's when Jack goes. He jams his body forward, his legs straight then pumping, arms shielding his face as he hits the patio doors' wooden center with both forearms. He blasts the doors open, shooting his body out onto the short wooden porch, and in the next moment he's in the yard going headfirst for the intruder's knees.

Like a quarterback evading the blitz at the last second, the shooter tries to shuffle to his side, but Jack grabs him around both thighs with an arm and a shoulder and drives him down hard onto his back.

The gun goes off, its silencer lisping into the night. The guy chops at Jack around the shoulder, grazing his ear with the butt of the gun, and then Jack feels the hard gunstock bounce off the back of his neck. Jack tries for a better hold on his attacker's legs, and the guy scrambles backward, turning and crawling on all fours for a few yards before he straightens up into a run, just as Jack is standing, uncomfortable in his socks on the wood chips.

In a moment, the guy's gone. Jack hears the sound of feet going faster than he can run in his socks, tearing out away from the yard in the dark along the side of his house.

"Fuck," he says, shaking the dirt and chips off. He scrambles back across the deck and into the living room, vaults the couch, and rushes to the side door.

In the darkness, from his side porch, Jack can hear feet pounding down the driveway. Then he sees the shooter under the streetlight more than thirty feet away: a man with light brown hair and a medium build, running down the last five feet of the driveway into the street to a new yellow Mustang retro redo, its backside as recognizable as anything on the road— pushed into the air like a lonely whore's.

The shooter takes a last look back and then hurries into the car. Jack wants to yell something after him. A threat? *Something*. But he doesn't. As the car starts up, a puff of exhaust comes from the center of the bumper, and then, in a flash of taillights and peeling rubber, it's gone. Jack hasn't even made it off the porch. He momentarily considers chasing the car down on his Ducati, but shirtless and without shoes he wouldn't get far.

Maybe he should start sleeping with his shoes on, Jack thinks. That, or start sleeping somewhere else.

2

Back inside, Jack checks the patio doors: nothing broken but the glass. He was sloppy, coming home and not checking on something as obvious as whether the doors were locked—especially when he'd come home to a note from a cop on the table—the second disturbing item—and his bed burned to the ground.

He's lucky the guy didn't just walk in and kill him in his sleep. Jack slinks back to the couch and sits down, lights a cigarette to try to relax.

At six-thirty, he gives up on sleeping. He's had two cups of coffee and the only thing left is to put himself in the shower. So he does.

He dresses in a pair of dark linen pants, the ones he'd wear if he were in L.A. for a lunch meeting, and a striped button-down shirt, clothes good enough to make the rest of him—the grown-out hair and the motorcycle tan—look respectable. He runs a brush through his hair, even adds some old leave-in conditioner that he finds under the sink. The effect is a shaggy Pat Riley: his hair brushed back and barely under control, eager to blast out on its own.

By seven-thirty he's in the Mustang Fastback, a vintage '66

K-code, listening to it idle in the garage. He's inspected the monster under the hood, and now he revs the engine to hear its roar, to see if the old car did okay by itself these past six weeks. It sounds just fine—as angry and aggressive as ever.

The Fastback is still in mint condition except for the three bullet holes along the left side: two in the back panel and one in the door. As Jack eases out of the driveway, he looks down at the seat next to him where he's tossed the note from Sergeant Mills Hopkins, his old friend on the San Francisco police force.

Jack's across the Golden Gate Bridge in time to get caught in the worst of the morning traffic. He takes his cell phone out of the glove box and turns it on. Six weeks and he hasn't missed it. It starts beeping right away, telling him he's got new voice messages. He turns it off, tucks it under his seat.

He weaves his way through the Presidio, goes down Lombard, and takes Van Ness toward Bryant and the Hall of Justice. He finds a place to park and feeds some quarters into the meter. They've got the metal detector routine going so hardcore at the entrance that Jack has to remove even his belt to get in. On the fifth floor, he walks down a familiar hall to see the same receptionist sitting at the same desk. This time she doesn't even ask Jack who he's here to see.

"Mr. Palms," she says. "The sergeant will be glad to see you." She points Jack straight back toward Hopkins's office. "Do you think you could..." She holds out a small black notebook, open to a blank page, and extends a pen. She thanks him as he signs, tells him she "loved him" in *Shake 'Em Down*.

Jack angles his way through the desks in the big squad room, drawing a stare from one of the cops who's in this early, and heads back to a small, separate room. The door reads sgt. mills hopkins. Jack knocks twice.

Hopkins barks.

Jack opens the door and there's Sgt. Hopkins sitting behind his desk, a phone at his ear and a yellow legal pad in front of him. His desk is littered with stacks of paper and behind him is the same big wall of postings that was here the last time Jack paid a visit. Hopkins wears a checked shirt, tight around his gut, and has grown a mustache.

"Call you back." Hopkins hangs up the phone and stands to greet Jack, a heavy movement that creaks both his desk and his chair. "Jack motherfucking Palms," he says, extending his hand. "The big movie star. Glad you could bring your ass in."

"Glad to see you grew out the 'stache. They give you your last merit badge for that thing?"

Jack reaches to shake Hopkins's hand, not sure he really wants to, and at the last moment, Hopkins reaches out to slap him. He moves like a big cat—a lot faster than you'd expect—and Jack manages only a partial dodge. The slap lands square on his neck.

Hopkins breaks into a smile.

"Yeah, Jack. It's *almost* good to see you." Hopkins sits down, looks over the materials on his desk, and flips to a new page on his yellow legal pad. His face goes cold. "Hell of a day for you to make your appearance, though. Hell of a day."

"How about we start with why you'd break into my house to leave a note on my kitchen table—"

"Try locking your doors, asshole. Your back door was unlocked, so I went in. You answer your phone, it saves me the trip."

"I'll try to remember that. Whatever I can do to keep you out of my life."

Hopkins nods. He takes a freshly sharpened pencil out of the can on his desk. "Let's get to that in a minute, okay? Truth is, this day is fucked up and it connects to you. Not even nine-thirty and it's fucked beyond saving. Not good for the Hall."

"Try me. I've been up since three when someone shot at me."

Hopkins closes his eyes and then opens them and regards Jack. It's the first time Jack's ever seen him look like he cares. He makes a pronounced gesture of looking around the room, finishes by raising his eyebrows and tugging an ear lobe. It's either a sign for Jack to steal second or to be careful because others might be listening.

Jack nods.

"One of our own turned up dead this morning. They're saying he offed himself in his car. Found him parked at the mall in Walnut Creek."

"I'm sorry," Jack says, "but—"

Hopkins holds up his hand to cut Jack off. "And it gets worse." He looks down as he says the next part. "A sixteen-year-old girl was found in his backseat. Hands tied, *naked*, marks on her legs like she'd been tortured."

Hopkins waves his hand over the desk as if he's trying to get rid of a bad smell. "She was dead." Now he looks up at Jack. "You want to tell that to the guy's wife? The mother of his kids? Think that's a good call? How about calling the girl's parents?"

Jack waits for what's next.

"Thank Christ I didn't have to call them."

Jack looks at the surface of the desk. The faster he gets out of here, the better. "Let's get to why you wanted to see me."

Hopkins's nostrils go big as he takes a hard breath for a two-count, and then a new look comes over his face: calmer, if only by a little.

"*He* was what I wanted to discuss with you. Our dead cop is the guy you fingered from that mess at the Coast, the cop with Tony Vitelli and the Russians."

"O'Malley." Jack still remembers the name from when Vitelli introduced them. "So it's a bad cop going out with the trash. Who cares?"

Hopkins gives a short laugh and shakes his head. "You know, Jack, it should be that easy. But a couple of things are more complicated here. There's more we need to discuss."

"So discuss."

Hopkins frowns, looks around the office again. "I been looking hard at O'Malley since you dropped the dime, back before your little vacation." He waves his index finger around in a circle, as if he's swirling a cheap drink. "We brought in that bald Russian, did our best to pin a case on him, but he walked. Motherfucker lawyered up like a politician and skated on illegal duress. Know why?" Hopkins smiles a big fake smile.

"Maybe I had a little something to do with it."

"Ah, yeah. But I watched O'Malley, and nothing came out right. He's been working something—something big. A stakeout in North Beach that involves some hinky shit."

"Hinky?"

"Like the girl in his backseat. But also a special direct line to the commissioner. I can't even get a straight answer on what he was really working."

A knock comes from Hopkins's door, and Jack can see the silhouette of a big cop through the smoked glass. Hopkins makes a face. "Come in!"

A stocky Asian with a blue shirt and tie pushes his head into the office. He's got his hair spiked on top and shaved on the sides. On the side of his neck, Jack can see a few wisps of hair flaring out. He eyes Jack as if he's putting some pieces together, figuring things out. "Meeting in ten," he says.

Hopkins tells him he'll be there, and the other cop closes the door.

"Morning meeting, Jack. Today's going to be a live one. On top of all this, we got Walnut Creek saying it's their case."

Jack turns to the door again, checking the glass for shadows. "Why'd he look at me like that?"

"Matsumoto?" Hopkins raises his eyebrows, then his shoulders. "That one's on you, pal."

"How about his hair? Can you explain that mullet?"

"Not that either." He frowns. "People are going to be pissed at this meeting. Can you imagine trying to keep this story out of the press?"

"But they're your old friends, aren't they?"

Hopkins shoots Jack a hard look. "Even if I could have enjoyed the story they did on you and the mess you made of your marriage and your acting career, there was nothing I could have done to stop them if I tried. Fact is, Jack, you created that whole damn mess by yourself. You and your lovely ex-wife. At some point, you're going to have to accept that."

Jack bites his lip. Part of him knows the cop is right.

"What I'm saying—" Hopkins puts his finger to his legal pad.

"We have to talk about this later. Where can I find you this afternoon?" Hopkins stands up and offers his hand to Jack across the table. "Don't say it here. Call my cell later and leave a message."

Jack stands and, confused, takes the cop's hand and gives it a brief shake.

"We didn't even get to the real reason I came in. I wanted to tell you about some douche bag trying to shoot me last night in my yard."

Hopkins's eyebrows go up. "Yeah, I'd like to discuss that."

"Ah, yeah," Jack says. Behind him, there's another knock at the door.

"All right," Hopkins calls. "I'm coming!" He's already walking around the desk, straightening his tie, and angling Jack toward the door.

"Later. Listen, you watch your back. We'll talk this afternoon."

3

Jack walks up Bryant and around the corner to where he parked his car. He sees the now-familiar craters along the driver's side, the three bullet holes, and puts his finger to the one on his door. Its smooth metal cradles his fingertip.

"Shit."

He wants to get them fixed or work on them himself, but with the bald Russian out and around, the burned bed, and the shooter in his yard, he shouldn't be cruising the city. He should be lying low.

Jack gets in and starts the Fastback, pulling his cell phone out from under the seat. It's not time to go looking for answers; it's time he found a place to disappear.

He takes a decent room at the St. Francis downtown, up on the sixteenth floor. It's not the Regis, but that suits Jack fine. He's coming around to the fact that the house in Sausalito might not be exactly him either.

His days of enjoying the view, of trying to live the calm life for the past three years while he built himself back up piece by piece, don't fit anymore. He doesn't want to go back to the hard work on his body, the same boring routine. Since he got started with Ralph a few months back, he's been cruising, and part of him wants to keep rolling with that instead of building every step of the way.

If he's going to keep on like this, though, he has to get his head on straight and start paying closer attention to the details. He's glad he took the time to put a few boards over the broken glass on his back doors and pack some clothes into a gym bag.

Looking out the hotel window down onto Post Street, Jack sees the cars and the foot traffic and knows he can get used to the action of the city again.

He finds his cell phone in one of his jacket pockets and turns it back on. The familiar graphic of two friendly hands joining lights up the screen, then its song starts chiming. Jack waits for the number of messages to show and then, impatient, he calls his voicemail.

He hasn't checked his messages or answered his phone for six weeks. The eight messages start with calls from Mills Hopkins, then an old one from Joe Buddha asking if Jack is okay and where he is. Next he's got a call from Victoria: not a happy one, worse than her usual annoyed tone, wanting him to call her back as soon as possible because she "really needs him for something." He figures she called back after this but wouldn't leave another message. Typical her: needing him but not wanting to show it too much. The truth is, Jack's glad not to hear more from her.

There's a message from the guy at the bank, his mortgage broker, the same guy who used to call and harass him to pay up, thanking him for the payment, late and for more than he owed. Now the broker says if there's anything else he can do for Jack that Jack should feel "perfectly welcome to call."

The last calls are another one from Buddha and one more

from Sergeant Hopkins, saying that he's concerned about where Jack is and whether he's all right, but that he'd know if anything happened because he'd recognize Jack's ugly mug on any John Doe that turned up. Hopkins ends his last message with "Shit, Jack. If you don't give a call sometime, I'm going to have to go over to your casa and let my ass in to look around."

Jack puts the phone on the bedside table. He made the right decision to leave it behind, but now that he's back, he'll have to start belonging to the city again, its game.

He lies down on the bed and closes his eyes, tries to meditate away some of the stress from the morning, but when he does, he sees the open spaces of Montana and Nevada, the mountains in Wyoming—the pictures all there on the backs of his lids, almost as if he were still on his bike.

Then his phone rings, and Jack opens his eyes. He looks at the clock and sees it's almost five. He sits up and shakes his head, realizes he's been sleeping in his clothes for the past four or five hours. Hasn't even moved. The phone rings again.

"Okay," he says.

He knows who'll be on the other end: Hopkins, the only one Jack told he'd be at the St. Francis. And Jack knows he'll be ready to talk.

"Yeah," Jack says, picking up the phone. "I'll be down in a minute."

"That's good," Hopkins tells him. "I'm in the bar."

4

Jack gets downstairs in five minutes, not fast enough to see Hopkins drink his first martini. He finds the cop fishing an olive out of an empty glass with his finger.

"That good, huh?" Jack asks, pulling out the chair next to Hopkins at the bar.

"A shit day. Press was all over this."

"And?"

"And shut up. Sit down and order a drink."

The bartender looks at Jack as he fills a shaker with ice for Hopkins's second martini. "Just a seltzer with lime for me."

Hopkins looks at Jack for a moment, starts to say something, then waves his hand through the air as if it's not worth it. Jack knows it *isn't* worth it; they have bigger things to discuss.

"Walnut Creek took it, O'Malley's case. But that's not even the worst."

"Okay."

"The worst is someone above me *gave* it to them, passed it right off. The whole thing smells like shit, Jack. A big shit burger."

"Nice image. Talk to me about how *I* fit into this. Because I'm still pissed about someone trying to shoot me."

Hopkins puts his hand over his eyes, massages his face for a few seconds, long enough for the bartender to finish making the second martini and set it down on a napkin.

"Yeah," he says. "How about because this *involves* you. You're a part of it, Jack. As soon as you fingered O'Malley. Soon as I busted you out and you started owing me favors. Now, listen." He taps the bar with his index finger. "The first part is this weird stakeout in North Beach that O'Malley was on. Someone high up put him on it. I can't even rate a look."

"So somehow I owe you favors?"

"You got it. The covered-up part involves more young girls like the dead one in O'Malley's car. Some kind of porn, sex-slave, prostitution ring that no one on the force is supposed to have heard of. That seem weird to you?" Hopkins doesn't wait for Jack to answer. "And now SFPD can't investigate this murder. No one's looking into the connection to North Beach, because none of us on this side of the Bay can work on O'Malley's death."

The bartender sets a lowball glass in front of Jack. This place is all class: dark wood, low lights, a window looking out onto the busy street outside. There are a few other people drinking at tables, but Jack and Hopkins have the bar to themselves.

"Plus it's not suicide. More we find out, the weirder it gets." Hopkins fondles the thin stem of the martini glass. "The guys who found the car heard *two shots*, and O'Malley's gun only fired one of them—not the one that killed him."

"So go find out who did. Isn't that what you guys do?"

Hopkins takes a long sip of his drink, long enough that the olives bounce once against his mustache, and then sets it down. "You listening to me? This is a bigger problem than just

O'Malley. One that goes up the force. Higher than I want to know."

"But?"

Hopkins nods. "But we've got to uncover it, right? Fuck if I don't have eighteen months left to retirement and could probably walk clean away from this, but it looks too dirty to leave. Not that I even care so much about O'Malley. He got what he deserved."

"He's dead, and I'm alive. Let's talk about my burned bed. What the fuck is that about?"

"Because what I think this all means is that we have some legitimate police officials, ones with big pull, associating with a known prostitution ring in North Beach and helping it stay under wraps. You know, your basic big-time civil-corruption type shit. And that we can't have."

Jack tastes his seltzer: nothing. Useless.

Hopkins sits back and grips his belt with both hands, pulls it up. "Yes, Jack. *We* have a problem with this, and *we* won't let it stand."

Hopkins puts his hand in front of Jack's face. "You listening to me?"

"What is this *we*?"

Hopkins laughs once. He takes another pull from the martini. "You saying you don't owe me? After all that shit I helped you with, after me keeping you *and* Junius Ponds out of jail—"

"I didn't—"

"Just so he can get killed. Not to mention your *duress* job on the Russian drug lord."

"I didn't have anything to do with those deaths," Jack says. "Is what I would say."

"Whatever, Palms." Hopkins waves his hand across the bar. "Half our suspects shoot themselves to shit in Tony Vitelli's. You leave me Alexi, one asshole Russian, and not enough to make anything stick on his ass?"

"This is my fault?"

"*And* I let you get away to have a nice vacation with your warlord pals and their coke buy, which yes, I know did happen. You going to make me go on, Jack, or should I just take you downtown to the Hall and we'll get this all *really* squared away?"

Hopkins looks at Jack for a long moment, maybe ten seconds, and then picks up his martini and drains off what's left, rolling both olives into his mouth.

Jack waves to the bartender. "Talisker." He points to the top-shelf scotch, the last one from the left. "Rocks."

The bartender smiles as he pulls out a new lowball glass and spins it right side up without looking. He starts for the bottle.

"That's right, Jack, now you're talking. Seeing what we have on our hands here."

"And by our you mean—"

"That's right, buttercup." Hopkins claps Jack hard on the back. "*You* and *me*, motherfucker."

5

The bartender sets Jack's drink down in front of him: four ice cubes and two fingers of good scotch. He'd had a few drinks on the road, but being off the wagon still makes Jack uneasy. He's an addict, after all. Maybe that doesn't mean everything in this world, but it should. He lifts the glass and takes a long swallow, pulls back his lips at the taste and feels the air on his teeth. "You going to protect me?"

"I'll do everything in my power."

"And then what will you do?"

Hopkins nods at the bartender's suggestion of another martini. He brings out a manila folder from the briefcase that's been sitting next to him on the floor and drops it onto the bar. When he flips it open, Jack sees a picture of O'Malley with half his head blown into next Tuesday. "Here's our boy. Remember the face?"

"What's left of it."

"Yeah. O'Malley was carrying a standard .38 revolver. Even at point-blank range, that caliber bullet doesn't do this. So who shot the gun that did?"

Hopkins slides the picture aside for another: this one of a young girl, hands cuffed in front of her with a set of nylon flex ties. Jack's seen the flex ties before: They're the kind cops always have on hand, but the bouncers at the Mirage and the Coast also used them. Her throat is slit.

The photo is taken from outside the car and the girl is laid out across the backseat. She's naked other than the cuffs. Clean shaven head to toe. "Shit. That's a sad thing to see."

"No blood around her." Hopkins points to the girl's neck and the seat around her head. "Dry as new leather."

"She wasn't killed in the car."

"Good job." Hopkins pushes the picture over to reveal another shot, this one of the car from the passenger's side. Jack stops, freezes in the fraction of a second it takes him to recognize the yellow Mustang redo.

"Motherfuck!" Jack stabs the picture with his finger. "This is the same car."

"Same as—"

"Last night. The dude who shot at me! I chased him out of my backyard, and this is the yellow piece of shit he drove off in."

"See what I'm saying, Jack?" Hopkins reaches out to touch Jack, but Jack moves away.

"Why's O'Malley shoot at me then wind up dead?" Jack turns to Hopkins. "Did I mention someone torched my bed? Burned the shit out of it right down to the rug?"

Hopkins looks at the car and then looks at Jack.

"If O'Malley took a shot at you—"

"Shots."

"—then you're in deep, pal."

"Shit."

"So it's *we*. Whether you like it or not." Hopkins smiles, and

22

Jack thinks he's going to be sick. He takes a long pull off the scotch. Maybe too long. He coughs, feels the room drop a little.

"Calm down, man. Go easy. What time was this?"

"Close to three. What time did they find the car?"

"Four-thirty."

Jack shakes his head, takes another hit of scotch. "Motherfuck."

Hopkins sits back, raises his glass as if making a toast. "How can we know the paths of our lives, Jack?"

Jack sees Hopkins take a drink, and he wants to walk out, check his car out of the garage, and head east, never looking back. But he knows if he did, he'd *never* be able to stop looking back— over his shoulder, behind his car, everywhere; he'd always be afraid of someone coming at him.

"How's a cop afford a car like that? Where's he get the money? These are the questions you might ask."

"Fuck you, Mills."

Hopkins flips the folder closed. "In yellow, too. Motherfucker wasn't afraid of attention."

"What is that thing? Some kind of new Mustang? It doesn't have *half* the balls of my '66."

Hopkins opens the folder again and looks at the car. "Come on, Jack," he says, turning the folder and the picture toward him. "That's a nice fucking car."

Jack snorts. "Sure."

"Don't you read your *Car and Driver*? It's a Saleen. The fanciest take on the new model."

"Must've let my subscription run out." He closes the folder and looks at Hopkins. "Let me guess, though: You subscribe in a package deal with *Cock and Balls*?"

Hopkins nods, tips his new drink at Jack. "That's my boy. You starting to feel better?"

"So what the fuck was this guy doing in my backyard?"

Hopkins shakes his head as he drinks, and Jack can only assume the worst: that O'Malley knew Jack had fingered him or that he was sent by someone else—the Russian.

"You said you were watching him."

"You know," Hopkins says, "the shit of all this is I actually do give a fuck. I never got into this business for the money." He takes a fast drink. "The thought of my own force, my department, being corrupt all the way to the top gives me the *agida* worse than you could guess."

"That's nice of you."

"Right here." Hopkins touches his heart and laughs. "It sounds dumb, but that's how it is. This thing's too big for me to walk away from."

Jack takes a pull off the scotch. It's bitter and it burns. He closes his eyes for a second. "So don't walk away, then."

Hopkins's lower lip rises, sucking up his mustache; he scowls but starts a slow nod at the same time. Then he taps his knuckles on the bar. "That's what I've been getting to, Jack. Fucking Walnut Creek investigates this shooting?" He laughs. "No way we let that pass. One of us gets killed, even one like O'Malley, we stop at nothing to find out who did it. And someone high up broke that code."

"Go get him."

"Our hands are tied. We need someone who's not on the force to do some investigating. A couple of us, call us the Concerned Citizens of the Police, we want to hire *you*, Jack. I put the funds together to back you."

"You want to hire me?"

Hopkins nods. "You did a good job with that Vitelli shit, whether I like it or not. I recognize you left me a pretty good package with that Russian. He *is* the primary new supply line of coke in this town. And when I say we'll stop at nothing, I mean we'll even go to unconventional means."

"That's some shit."

"Right, Jack. *You* are our unconventional means. Fact is, you're the guy on the outside I know. You can do this like we can't."

Jack looks hard at his scotch. He runs his fingers along the side of the glass. Part of him doesn't know, part of him wants to run, and part of him wants to get his ass to Walnut Creek to see what he can find.

"Plus there's the shit at your house. You work this through, it benefits you. You see it cleaned up and know where you stand." Hopkins pauses a beat, his eyebrows rising. "I got a friend in Walnut Creek we can trust. He'll set you up for a look at the car."

The bartender slides a receipt on the bar toward Hopkins, goes back to polishing glasses while he watches a small TV above the bar.

Jack swallows another pull of scotch and turns to Hopkins. "If I do this, you keep me updated. I want total access to whatever you know."

"Whatever I have, it's yours."

"Even if Walnut Creek is doing the investigation, you find out what you can about whatever I need. And if I do this, I'm bringing in help. I get the man I need, he's going to need something from you, something good."

Hopkins nods, doesn't ask who Jack means—a good sign.

"Someone to watch your back is a good idea. There's money for him too. Don't you worry."

Hopkins waves the bartender over and asks for water.

Jack looks at the scotch. It's time to go to work, to tighten the strings. He pushes the drink away and picks up his seltzer with lime. Now he wants a smoke.

Hopkins raises his water glass, clinks it against Jack's. "So we work this?"

"I'm staying here at the St. Francis. The department will pick up that tab?"

"That I can do." Hopkins taps his billfold. "I'll give them my witness account before I leave."

"Good." Jack knocks a cigarette out of his pack and taps it against the bar. "Tell me where to start."

6

Up in his room, Jack drops onto the bed, a hotel drinking glass and a lighter in his hand. He props his head on two pillows and lights a cigarette, knowing it's illegal in the hotel but beyond caring. The smoke will smooth out the burn of the scotch and the nerves he's got from Hopkins's proposition. He takes a long drag, blows smoke straight up in the air like the assassin in his favorite French movie, *Le Samouraï*.

Someone coming after him isn't anything Jack likes to think about, but Hopkins hiring him to do this job makes him sit up a little, even smile. This is the closest he's felt to being a part of something in three years, the closest to having a career, actually being some*thing*. He knows he's not cut out to be a fitness guru or someone's personal trainer, and he's still in the Hollywood deep freeze, and the NFL's not chasing after his thirty-two-year-old ass. So what is he? Fact is, whatever *this* is, it's something. Mills fucking Hopkins, ball-breaking cop, thinks he did a good enough job on Vitelli that he wants to *pay* to see what Jack can find out about O'Malley's death.

Damn.

Just the thought of getting hired gets Jack to snap straight up off the bed and kick his feet onto the floor. He ashes his smoke onto the carpet and stamps it down. Any fines or fees and the SFPD can get that tab. Jack wishes he'd booked a suite.

And now he doesn't think about leaving San Francisco. The facts change just like that.

He takes a last drag and then stubs out his cigarette against the side of the drinking glass. Next he picks up his cell and dials Joe Buddha.

Buddha's wife comes on the line, saying "Yes, hello?" in a small voice.

"Hey, Yuko. This is Jack Palms, a friend of Bu—uh, John's."

"Yes," she says. "Mr. Jack Palms from *Shake 'Em Down*. The movie star." She laughs.

Buddha comes on the line, says he's finishing up his afternoon meditation.

"I'm back from the road," Jack says, and brings Buddha up-to-date on the condition of his house and the shooter in his yard.

"Your bed, Jack? That's not right."

"No shit."

"You're not home, are you? Want to come by and stay here for a while?"

"No, thanks. I'm at a hotel. You got anything on Victoria?"

"You don't need to worry about Victoria burning your bed. She's been making the rounds in LA again, got some new boy toy, the guy who just wrapped *El Camino Royale*, that picture about the family of Mexican bank robbers with the trar. Word is it'll gross more than fifty mil."

"Yeah. I saw the ads for it: 'Like James Bond, only more Mexican.' Real nice."

Buddha coughs. "Yeah. She's doing her thing again.

Whatever that means for her health and well-being."

"Right. We don't need to get into that. You hear anything about Freeman Jones?"

"Yeah. He's been around the new spots a little. I saw him in Japantown one time at the Golden Pagoda, but he's not there like he used to be. There's a new strip club in North Beach that's getting a lot of action. You might find the big man around there."

"Appreciate it, Joe. See you in the movies."

Jack flips his phone closed, tosses it onto the bed, and stands up. In the full-length mirrors beside the TV, he can see he looks like hell. His clothes are wrinkled from sleeping in them, and his hair looks like he needs another shower. For where he's heading, he's going to need to look good.

7

With a clean pair of dark linen pants and a crisp white shirt on, Jack heads down to the lobby to get a cab for North Beach. A guy like Freeman, if you can find the *area* he's in, you can find him. Not like he's easy to forget, not with his size and the big tattoos across half his face.

By the time the cabdriver asks Jack where he wants to be let off, they're at the intersection of Columbus and Broadway, more or less the center of North Beach. "This is good," Jack says, reaching for his wallet.

On Columbus, the night is starting to come alive. People stand smoking outside the bars, already waiting in lines. A few kids call out Jack's name, saying "*Shake this man down!*" and pointing at him with both hands like they hold six-shooters. He got recognized on the road a few times, in Phoenix and Las Vegas especially, but it was never anything bad, only an autograph or a kid wanting to take his picture. Here, people are aggressive when they're drunk. They make Jack tense. Without the Czechs, he has no protection, no entourage to fend people off; he's out on his own, shaking hands and smiling for camera-phone mug shots whether he wants to or not.

He jumps the line at a club that looks hipper than most, one with a blue neon sign above the front entrance, a word written in unreadable script. The guy behind the red ropes is bigger than anyone Jack's seen in a while, but not bigger than Freeman. He's got a gelled-up flattop, tanning-booth skin, and big jaw muscles clenching at his temples as he chews a wad of gum.

Through a smirk, the guy says "What can I do to you?" in a British accent. Jack's confused for a moment; he expected the guy to sound like a typical thick-neck.

"You know me?" Jack says.

The bouncer shrugs. "I seen you in a movie. You know."

"Good. You know Freeman Jones?"

"Jets lineman. Not bad. Yeah. I seen him around."

Jack still can't get over the accent, but he pushes forward. "Know where I can find him?"

A guy sticks his ID in the bouncer's face, and the big man shoves him back into the line with one arm. "You wait," the bouncer says. "Ever hear of patience?"

A strong hip-hop beat thumps from inside the club.

"Sorry about that." The bouncer looks at Jack and closes one eye like he's thinking hard while a suit goes to the front of the line, looks at the ID of the guy the bouncer pushed away.

"He's big," Jack says. "Samoan. Got a tattoo on half his face."

The bouncer nods. "Yeah. Yeah. He bounces at the Pretty Lady. Few blocks up Broadway." He points toward the Bay. "That's where I seen him."

"Thanks." Jack hits the guy on the shoulder.

"Tell him he should've played two more years. Pussy move to retire like that." The bouncer tilts his chin at Jack. "Speaking of pussy, what's up with your next movie?"

Jack shrugs and throws the bouncer a wave. Answering the sequel question got old two years ago. But people still want to know. He walks back up to Broadway and turns right. Up the block he can see signs for three or four clubs, and down at the end of these, across the street, a tall vertical sign in the shape of a woman's leg reads: the pretty lady.

Someone walks right into Jack, bumps him hard on the shoulder. The guy's on his cell phone and not paying attention. He turns, glares at Jack, and says something into the phone in another language, one that sounds thick and full of consonants. Then his eyes narrow. The guy has dark hair, wears a gray suit with a white shirt, its collar out over the suit's lapels. No tie.

They stare at each other for a breath and then keep on. When Jack looks back, Gray Suit says something into his phone and slides it closed. He stands in place, eyeing Jack.

Ten yards later, Jack crosses the street and looks back: Gray Suit's no longer there. Jack looks up and down the block, doesn't see him anywhere now.

Up the block and past the second club, Jack sees Freeman standing in front of the Pretty Lady, arms folded, hair pulled back into a ponytail that makes the tattoo on his face seem even more prominent. Jack can't tell what it represents; it's a pattern, like the black tribal tattoos he's seen on people's shoulders and backs, but this one covers the whole right side of Freeman's face and creeps down his neck into his shirt. It's got to be something from Samoa, representing where Freeman's from, but *still*. When he was in the NFL, they called him the Beast and Freakman because of it.

Two other bouncers outside the Pretty Lady wear suits, but

Freeman has on black sweats, a baggy velour combination with a zip-up top. He sees Jack from ten feet away and a big smile cracks his mug.

"Oh, shit," Freeman says, stepping over the club's ropes to come toward Jack. "Look who's back in the motherfucking city!"

Jack smiles. He can't help himself.

Freeman claps hands with Jack and pulls him in for a big one-armed hug. "It's good to see you. Good you back around."

"How are you?" Jack coughs after the tight embrace and backs a step away from the bigger man to get his breath. Even at six foot three—or six four on a good day—Jack has to look up to meet eyes with Freeman, who must stand six foot seven or eight. He's all size, all bulk, and definitely hasn't gotten any smaller since Jack last saw him. "How's the leg?"

"I was on a cane for a little while there, but that gave me something to hit people with, you know? Scared the motherfuckers."

Jack nods. Freeman needing a cane to scare someone has to be a joke.

"I'm all right now. Standing on my own two. Not running any five-second forties, but shit, those days *been gone.*"

It's hard for Jack to imagine anyone as big as Freeman ever running a five-second forty, but he's not about to question him on it.

"So, yeah, I'm doing fine."

Jack nods toward the club. "And I see you got some new employment?"

Freeman makes a face. "Shit with Junius was definitely more free-form, you know? We did our own thing. But this all right. Not too hard."

"Anything else taking up your time?"

Freeman shakes his head. He pats his biceps like he's cold. "This my deal now. Business reshuffles, things change. I'm trying not to be too involved with the traffic."

"So you wouldn't want to get into something with me?"

Freeman looks back at the other bouncers in front of the club: both suits, both chewing gum and wearing dark sunglasses. Nobody's gone inside since Jack got close. It's the slow part of the night, will probably stay slow until the regular bars and clubs close at two. Freeman turns back to Jack, his eyebrows pressed together. "Like what?"

Jack shrugs. "What time you here until?"

"Four, five. I could stand to get involved in something," Freeman says. "But it has to pay. You got money?"

"Money's a lock. I just need someone to watch my back."

Freeman smiles. "Yeah. I can see that. You lost a few pounds out on the road, huh?" He catches Jack's arm by the bicep and squeezes. "Yeah. You lost a little, didn't you? Better get back in that gym."

"Not like I can't handle myself, though." Jack throws a fake punch at Freeman's middle, and the big man reacts fast, knocks Jack's arm away before Jack can even pull it back.

"No," Freeman says. "But then you couldn't handle yourself before, as I remember. Out here in the *real* world, that is."

Jack tilts his head. "I do all right."

"Yeah." Freeman squeezes Jack's bicep a little harder. "But this ain't make-believe. This real-world shit, Jack. This what *I* get paid for. And I get paid well."

"That's why I came."

Freeman lets go of Jack's arm and fishes a business card from one of his pants pockets. "Call me tomorrow at this number. Not too early."

Jack goes through the motions as Freeman claps his hand again and pulls him in for the one-arm hug.

"When your next movie?" the big Samoan asks.

"Everybody with that question." Jack gives him a wave, turns, and, as he does, notices Gray Suit ducking into one of the pizza places up the block.

8

Jack keeps walking, makes a right on Columbus and heads toward Washington Square. He needs to think, an act he does best with his legs moving.

A block up Columbus, he starts to get a weird feeling like he's being watched. He ducks into a late-night coffee shop, one with fancy desserts along the counter. Through its front window, he sees Gray Suit standing in front of a bookstore, straining to look interested.

Jack heads out, crosses the street to double back on the guy. Up a block, he crosses back to the same side, checks to see if the suit is still at the window. He's not. The guy's completely gone. Jack stops.

"Shit," he says, then heads toward Broadway, planning to hop a cab and get his ass back to the hotel. But he considers what an encounter with Gray Suit would be like if the guy were to follow him to his hotel room. He stops again, caught by his own uncertainty, standing still on the cement, and decides to head back to the Pretty Lady, determined to hire Freeman right away.

Then, out of the corner of his eye, Jack sees Gray Suit across the street, walking straight at him. The guy disappears in a crowd of kids eating pizza, but then he's there again.

A chill touches every vertebrae down Jack's spine; he wonders if he should've made for the East Coast.

Instead, he takes out his cell and dials the number on Freeman's card.

"Free," he says, when the big man grunts his answer. "I got a dude tailing me. Coming your way. I want you to start working with me right now. I need you."

There's a pause on the phone, then Jack hears Freeman talking to someone at the club. When he comes back, he says, "Where you at?"

"Columbus and Grant. Check the dude in the gray suit not far behind me when you get close."

"On it."

Jack flips the phone closed. He doesn't see Gray Suit but keeps walking, knowing he's there somewhere.

When he reaches Broadway, Jack hears a voice over his shoulder. "Mr. Palms," it says in a thick accent. "Why don't you come with me? I would like chance to talk."

Jack turns to see an alley: dumpsters, some back entrances to restaurants and clubs. Gray Suit stands beside him, too close, holding a black revolver. A second guy steps in front of Jack. Another suit, this one in black but similar to the gray, like they came from the same cheap shop on Market.

Black Suit waves toward the alley. "Why don't we step in here."

Jack takes a last glance at the people in front of the clubs and a car going past—a police car. He tries to make eye contact with the cop in the passenger seat, but the cop's not watching, has his eyes to the windshield, intent. In a moment, the car's roof lights come on and the cops speed away.

Gray Suit smiles. The other one, too pale and with bad teeth like a row of overlapping tombstones, cracks his knuckles. "Like we tell you." He points down the alley.

What else can Jack do? He walks into the dirty alley. It's not a place he wants to go with two guys in slick suits and rough accents—especially with one of them holding a gun.

"So what's this about, fellas?" Jack asks, his hands raised, trying to stall for Freeman. "What can I help you with tonight? Maybe an autograph?"

The suits both laugh. "Ha," Black Suit says. "He is funny comedian, no?"

"No, André," the other one says and shrugs. "He not so funny as he think."

"What do we want with you, Jack Palms?" The one named André comes closer to Jack, touches the collar of his shirt. "These are nice clothes, Mr. Palms. You are dressed very nice. You go to the clubs?" He slaps Jack lightly on the side of the face once, then twice. "We too like these clubs." Then he slaps Jack again, harder.

"Do I know you guys?"

"No." André pushes Jack farther down the alley and comes after him. "You do and you also do not. But you know our friends. Yes. Them you do."

"You mean Vlade and Al?"

"Oh, no. These are not *our* friends."

Gray Suit comes forward, his gun trained on Jack, but the alley is tight; if Jack slides to his left four inches, André will block any possible shot.

"You guys wouldn't be friends with a big bald Russian fuck, would you?" Jack asks. "A dumb asshole who I last saw cuffed to a pool table?"

André hits Jack in the stomach, hard.

Hard, but not hard enough that Jack can't think straight. Still, it hurts like someone sapped half his energy. Pain runs down his legs. He doubles over, buying time to catch his breath.

"Yes, that is our friend whom you know," André says. "And if you keep up this joking, we will have more of these violences."

Jack shuffles over a couple of inches as he spits on the ground.

André pulls Jack's head up by his ear so the two of them see eye to eye. "Yes. We think you know our friend. And our friend, he *knows* you." Jack can feel the guy's breath hot on his face, smelling like pepperoni mixed with vodka. "How was your bed when you arrived at home from your *road trip*?" He pronounces "road trip" like it's the worst sexual act he can imagine.

"You two love birds know something about my bed?"

André nods, way too close now, lightly hitting Jack in the forehead with his own. He smiles wide, showing Jack his jagged teeth and more than a few nose hairs that need trimming. "We made your bed for you. Did you like that?"

"That was you fucks?" Jack counts his breaths. He wants to punch this shithead with everything he has. Anyone who comes into his house and burns his bed to the floor deserves nothing less.

"Ta ta," André says. "You should be more careful about whom you make angry. Your bed was present from Alexi Akakievich." He stabs Jack in the chest with a stiff finger. "That was your warning, Jack Palms. Alexi Akakievich is not usually so kind."

And that's when he hauls off and hits Jack under his ribcage, doubling him over again. Now suddenly nauseated and with a mouth full of saliva, Jack lets it go, leaving a stream of spittle and bile across André's leather shoes.

Jack catches his breath in time to see a right hook coming at his temple. He flinches so it lands on his shoulder instead. Gray Suit hasn't moved; he's still standing behind André, watching the action. Jack picks his spot: He punches André with an uppercut to the balls and runs into him, pushing him back toward his partner. Both of them fall back against the wall between a Dumpster and a line of garbage cans. The gun goes off, its muzzle pointed up into the night. Jack hears the ring in his ears that he knows too well and comes up swinging.

He throws wild punches, trying to get off enough of them to stun the Suits before someone starts shooting. A big right connects to Gray Suit's head. Jack punches him again in the face, a quick combo, and the guy smiles at Jack for a second. It's in this moment, after Jack has hit this guy with everything and produced a smile, that one thought rushes through Jack's mind: *Oh, shit.*

Gray Suit hits Jack with a chopping right that plants the butt of his revolver in Jack's cheek.

Jack gets his hands up, but the Suit hits him again, this time with a fast jab to the nose. The pain comes on like a wall of red.

Gray Suit says, "You are not so smart, Jack Palms." The square nose of the gun presses against Jack's temple. "And you have not learned to fight like in your movie. You are only actor. I can see now that the Hollywood effects are all the bullshit." He pulls Jack up by the hair so Jack is looking right at him. Jack can see the same smile, only more vicious now, a thin trickle of blood running down the side of the Suit's mouth.

To his left, Jack sees André straightening up, taking a few breaths to regain himself after the shot to his balls. Then he rushes at Jack, and Jack flinches, expecting the worst.

But instead of feeling André's bull rush, Jack hears a crash, then more of them—as if human bowling balls were knocking down garbage cans.

He looks up to see Freeman standing over a demolition derby of garbage and Suits. The big man grabs Gray Suit's gun hand and bites the guy's fingers until he screams. Freeman throws the gun to the ground, spits out something white—skin?—into the garbage, and shakes his head. Gray Suit freaks out, covers his hand, but not before Jack sees blood dripping down his wrist. André starts to get up, but Freeman kicks him once in the face, then stomps down hard on his ankle. André barely stifles a scream.

As Gray Suit starts to stand, still holding his hand, Freeman punches him in the temple. He buckles, and Freeman kicks him to the ground.

Then Freeman lifts Jack up by the shoulders, dropping him roughly on his feet. Jack touches his nose and looks at his hand: He's thankful it's not full of blood. He wipes his eyes.

"I'm okay."

A sound comes from the garbage cans as André starts to move. When André's half standing, Freeman stabs his neck with two pointed fingers. André coughs, grabs his Adam's apple, and doubles over, hacking on his own voice box. Freeman punches him in the side of the head with a left hand as big as a five-pound potato. The guy falls into the garbage cans again, hard. Gray Suit's standing, looking at his gun on the other side of Freeman.

"Yeah. There it is." Freeman nods at the gun.

The Suit looks at the gun and at Freeman, thinks it over for a second, and decides there's no way he's getting past Freeman. He pulls his friend upright, and they start shuffling toward Columbus.

"Should I stop them?" Freeman asks.

"Probably." Jack puts his hand over his nose again, feeling along its bridge to see if it's broken. "Whatever."

"You all right, bro?"

Jack opens and closes his eyes. "Yeah," he says. "I'll be okay. Just give me a minute." Jack shakes his head to clear it, spits some blood on the ground. Then he looks down the alley and sees the Suits are gone.

By the Dumpster, Freeman picks up the gun and looks it over—down the barrel and along its side. "Not a bad piece," he says. He looks at Jack, then back toward the street. "We need those two, we can find them. I seen them around from time to time." He comes over to Jack and offers him the gun. "You got to protect your interests."

"What took you so long?" Jack tries to keep a straight face. "I was just starting to kick some ass here. But, you know, I didn't want to be the only one having a good time." He takes the gun, slips it into the back of his pants.

"Not a problem, my man." Freeman pats Jack on the shoulder. "You can thank me later. I'm with you now; there'll be plenty of fun to go around."

"That's good."

Freeman grabs Jack's face with one hand and takes a careful look at his nose. "Your nose ain't even broken. You were a quarterback, you'd be thanking me."

"Thanks. What would Junius have said if he took a beating like that, had a guy put a gun to his head?"

"Junius?" Freeman laughs, then tilts his head to get another look at Jack. "Palms, my man, Junius would *never* let that shit happen. You got to take better care of yourself." He slaps Jack lightly across the cheek and heads to the mouth of the alley.

9

The next morning, Jack wakes up late and has a nice, full breakfast in the St. Francis's main dining room. He thinks about inviting Freeman to help him ring up the charges on Hopkins's credit card, but it's probably still too early for the big man. Their plan is to meet in the afternoon and go over to Walnut Creek.

Jack scours the newspapers while he drinks his coffee, but the facts don't add up: There's nothing about the girl in any of the papers.

After a lengthy description of O'Malley's car and the names of the detectives in Walnut Creek working the investigation, the piece in the *Chronicle* veers off to an interview with O'Malley's mother. She never wanted him to join the force, it turns out. "I wanted him to be a pharmacist or a doctor."

Apparently he'd even had a nice roast-beef dinner with her on the night of his death. So he was well fed when he came to Jack's house to kill him—a comforting thought.

The last paragraph of the article has one interesting fact: O'Malley had been on the SFPD's vice task force for the past four years.

After skimming the *Oakland Tribune* and the *San Jose Mercury News* for anything more and finding nothing, Jack hits the hotel gym to try to sharpen up as Freeman suggested. He knows he'll feel better after sweating some of the kinks out, something he didn't do nearly enough on the road.

After his shower, Jack finds a message from Mills Hopkins on his phone: the name and number of a guy in Walnut Creek who works at the car impound where O'Malley's Saleen is being held.

So a look at the car will be Jack and Freeman's first stop.

Freeman picks Jack up outside the hotel in Junius Ponds's silver Mercedes Benz. Jack has to wonder if it still has a trunk full of guns, but he doesn't bother to ask.

In the car, Jack fills Freeman in on what he knows about O'Malley's death and how the now-dead cop tried to put a bullet in him. When he tells Freeman about the Russians burning his bed, the big man's interest flares up.

"That's a big-time hit to burn down your bed, Jack. Sends a loud message."

"What's the message?"

"You fucked. They saying we can get at your ass where you sleep—*where you live.*" Freeman's eyes go big. "That's what that says."

"Lots of people know where I live. Didn't you read about me in the papers?"

Freeman laughs, a short loud grunt. "I don't read that shit, Jack. Fuck. Tabloids are there when I go to the supermarket, but I be reading the fitness magazines."

Jack looks at Freeman. The thought of a three-hundred-pound-plus NFL lineman with a tattoo on his face shopping at a supermarket surprises him. But everyone's got to buy food, right? Jack shakes it off, watches the cargo ships in the distance as Freeman drives across the Bay Bridge.

"That's why I got a hotel room."

"You feel safe there?"

"Saf*er*."

"Somebody lining you up, Jack, getting you set in they sights. This dude in your backyard, if he's working with them and then he gets dead, they really cared whether he completed the job." Freeman holds up a hand so Jack doesn't interrupt. "Plus, someone lined that fucker *up*." He shakes his head. "Planned that shit and then did him mob-style. It takes brass balls to kill a cop. Everyone knows that's fit to bring down the serious shit."

"Those dicks said they work for an old friend of ours. Guy from Vitelli's. That bald dude from the Coast."

"*Him?*"

"Some dude named Alexi Akakievich."

"Oh, shit." Freeman bites his lips for a moment. "That's the name of the other dude at the Coast?"

"Yeah. That's him."

"He is *large* in the city right now. You don't want to mess with him."

"That's why I've got you."

"Shit." Freeman makes a face, and this reaction does more to intimidate Jack than anything that happened last night in the alley. "Then we both have to watch our backs. And that means paying me extra."

Jack shrugs, figures it won't hurt to tell Freeman who's footing the bill. "O'Malley was SFPD, but they're not allowed to run the investigation. Walnut Creek called this because it happened in their mall, and no one at SFPD said boo. The top line called them all back."

"You saying?" Freeman follows the center lanes off the bridge to get onto 580. He eyes Jack, waiting for more. When his dark eyebrows go up, Jack nods.

Freeman looks back at the road. "So. We watching Walnut fucking Creek?"

"SF does like a hundred murder investigations a year, Walnut Creek more like six. Who does a better job?"

"Someone don't want this done right."

"Someone with pull. Word came down from on high. Right when the SF boys are about to roll out, they get told to stay home. That's how we come in: A cop gets killed, other cops want revenge, even if their hands are tied. They need a name."

Freeman ignores the road; he studies Jack's face as if he's trying to decide whether it's all a joke. "And they called *you*?"

Jack waves his hand at the dash, trying to get Freeman to acknowledge the other cars. "Hey, man, it's strange to me too. But they're paying, so we go take a look around, right?"

Freeman nods. "Shit. Long as they paying." He laughs, finally turns back to the road. Jack tries to hide his big intake of breath.

After that, they stay quiet. The Mercedes rolls through the maze, onto 580 and then to 24, heading toward the Caldecott Tunnel.

"But that's what I'm saying," Freeman says. "We push up against Alexi Akakievich, we could get some serious shit rained down. Word on the street is same as you just said—he's protected from the inside. Someone with power—on the police, the city council, who knows who else—be putting his dick in Akakievich's bitches. I'm not just saying—" Freeman shakes his head. "Let me tell you: In North Beach, you want that young, off-the-boat, white-girl pussy, you go to Akakievich. And I heard he got some clients high up in the city's food chain."

"So, Walnut Creek," Jack says.

Freeman shakes his head, keeping his eyes on the road. They're coming to the tunnel, and even in the middle of the afternoon, the traffic slows.

"Let me ask you," Jack says. "When you were with Junius, you barely said shit. Now you're talking like a normal person."

The big man snorts. "J liked it that way. You know? Strong and silent. He thought it made us more intimidating."

"You think that would work for us?"

"No. Anyone saw that movie you did, they won't be scared while you're around."

Jack studies Freeman's face and sees no smile, though it's hard to tell what's happening behind the tattoo. "You didn't like *Shake 'Em Down?*"

Freeman laughs. "Palms," he says, tilting his head, "that was actually some pretty good shit. Good as far as action goes." He shakes his head. "Shit. Take it easy. That's the other thing different now: I'm warming up to you. We getting to know each other."

He reaches over and claps his hand around the back of Jack's neck, squeezes. Jack tries to push the big hand away with his shoulder blades, but it doesn't move. Freeman laughs, massaging Jack's neck.

Jack hopes he can handle having this new friend.

10

At the impound lot, Freeman pulls up to a high chain-link fence, and even before they get out, a pair of big German shepherds charges up to the fence, barking, front paws up on the metal, incisors flashing. Then, just as suddenly, the dogs calm down, drop to the ground, all four paws in place as if they were in a show.

Jack opens his door to get out of the car.

He follows Freeman to the gate, where a wrinkled little man with shocks of white hair poking out from underneath a stocking cap walks up toward them. He removes a small, metal dog whistle from his mouth. When he sees Freeman, his face breaks into a smile.

"I hear they send a movie actor, but Shaw didn't say anything about ugly. Jeez!" The little man laughs.

Freeman grunts. "He must be talking about you, Jack."

"We came to see the Mustang, the yellow Saleen."

"Where you get tattoo?"

"Shut it, little man. Show us the car."

The guy unlocks the gate slowly, still laughing, and ushers the dogs away. He waves Jack and Freeman in, still holding a hand in front of the dogs to keep them calm.

"Caesar, Brutus, back to you house." The dogs turn and run away from the fence.

"So where's the car?"

"It here," the man says. "Just come in yesterday. Nice car, but a hole in it like I never see." He whistles.

"Yeah?" Jack says. He walks quicker, ahead of Freeman now. "What kind of hole?"

"You see. You see."

They come around a corner and Jack sees the Mustang. Now he can see the word saleen on the bumper, right below the license plate and above the centered twin exhausts. In a sea of taupe sedans, the yellow sports car is the hottest, loudest thing in the lot. But the little man's right—even from ten feet away, Jack can see the hole in the roof.

Jack hurries over. Looking through the hole, he can see that something big came through and tore its way out of the driver's-side door. Both holes are big enough to swallow a man's hand. "What did this? A hot baseball?"

Freeman shakes his head.

As Jack walks around the car, he can see the metal layers of the door, the torn leather, the window well. The front seat's covered in dried blood and white specks. Where the driver's window is cracked into a web, Jack sees a single brown hair caught in its center. The dashboard is a mess of little pieces—pieces of person and glass.

"Fuck," Jack says, turning away.

Freeman whistles. "*That* is one sweet ride. What's a cop doing driving something like this?"

Jack glances at the big man. "Sweet if you like piece-of-shit, retro-craze, wannabe redos. How's this thing compare to my '66?"

Freeman laughs. "Easy, man. Nothing personal."

"I'm just saying. Shouldn't even be called a Mustang."

"Well, it's lighter, same horsepower, more speed, probably handles a shitload better—"

"Save on gas," the little man adds.

"Look at this design. Total fucking rip-off."

Freeman walks the length of the car, running his finger along the curve of the roof. "Come on, Jack. This is a pretty nice car."

Jack nods at Freeman. "Fuck you." He hits the roof. "Tin. But what could go through a car door like this? Shit, through a whole car?"

Freeman comes up beside Jack. "Only a fifty. That's the one thing."

"A fifty?"

"A fifty-cal. It's a big-ass assault rifle. Big as fuck. They're around, but they're mostly military use. This one cop I know said he tried them out on the force, just to get a feel. The army used them in Desert Storm. Now they using them in Iraq. But these are illegal as shit over here."

"Especially in California," the old man says. "The Barrett rifle highly illegal here. But—" He shrugs. "You can buy online."

Freeman looks over at the little man. "Really?"

He nods. "I not shit you."

Freeman looks as if he's considering this, but doesn't say anything.

Jack asks, "So who's using this gun to tear up the guy's car?"

"Another question for the list."

Jack looks through the roof again: A huge amount of white matter and dried blood is caked against the driver's side door. It's worse than the mess in Ralph's bathroom. The windshield of the car is gone, smashed out, little pieces of glass across the floor, the dash, and in between the seats. The place with the least glass is the seats—where two people must have been sitting. "What knocked out the windshield?"

Freeman shakes his head. He bends his knees to get eye level with the driver's window and looks inside. "Judging by these two big-ass holes, we know the fifty didn't shoot through the glass. Shot could've come through the windshield from inside, weakened the glass and it popped in on itself." He shrugs. "That could be our second bullet."

"Or maybe the first."

"Right." He nods. "Did your cop tell you anything about this hole?" Freeman stands up and puts his hand through the car's roof. He wiggles his fingers.

"He didn't mention it. I saw a picture of the car from the passenger side, no view of the roof."

"You think they were hiding this until they could find anything about who did it?"

"Shit if I know." Jack walks around to the passenger side of the car and looks through the roof hole at the hole in the door, trying to judge the angle of the bullet that made the damage. He traces it out with his hand and looks up to picture an imaginary building, how high and where it'd have to be for someone to make the shot.

"How's someone shoot through the roof of a car and know what they're going to hit?" Jack asks. "You shoot at this angle, you couldn't possibly see O'Malley in the front seat."

"Spotter?"

The old man walks around the trunk of the car, looks in through the rear window. "Spotter would work," he says. "But you have a gun like this, you don't need worry too much about missing. It make easy shot."

Freeman moves to look at the backseat of the car, and Jack does the same from the other side. With the tinted windows. it's impossible to see the upholstery.

"Mind if I?" Jack reaches for the handle.

"Whoa. Hold on." Freeman comes around to Jack's side and pushes his arm back up into the sleeve of his jacket. He touches the door handle with the sleeve, opens it carefully.

"I know I don't want to get fingerprints on this fucker," Jack says. He takes a handkerchief out of his pocket and waves it in front of Freeman.

Freeman shrugs and pulls the door open. The passenger seat is already buckled forward to reveal the car's small backseat. Jack puts his head in to take a closer look at the leather and doesn't see any blood on it. It's clean, exactly as Hopkins said.

"Girl wasn't killed here."

Freeman grunts.

"And why would O'Malley put her in the backseat instead of the trunk? You'd be okay driving around with a girl's body, even with tinted windows?"

"Maybe he wasn't the one who put her in," Freeman says.

Jack nods. From the inside, he sees leather hanging down from the hole in the car's roof. Some of the roof's insides are visible, but only a few scraps of metal are bent in.

"You think a bullet could go through my Fastback like this?"

Freeman laughs. "Yes. Shit, Jack, this thing could shoot through a brick wall up to a half mile out."

Jack stands up, looks at Freeman.

"Seriously?"

Both of the other men nod. "Don't you read *Guns and Ammo*?"

"No," Jack says. "Must've let my subscription run out."

"But you still get *Cock and Balls*, right?"

Jack smiles, shakes his head.

The old man clicks his teeth. "You want to look in trunk?"

"Sure," Jack says. He moves around to the back and pops the trunk using his handkerchief. When he lifts the lid, he expects to find a grizzly scene with lots of blood. But he finds nothing, only gray felt, the well for a spare with the spare in it.

"This guy's trunk is cleaner than mine."

Freeman comes around to have a look. He nods. "Yeah, that's about as clean as I'd keep my trunk if I had this car."

"Anything in the glove box?"

Freeman's already moving around the car. He uses his sleeve again.

"Nothing."

"Of course, if they find things in this car, the police keep," the old man says.

Jack nods. Freeman slams the door closed. "Time to ask your friend in SF some more questions."

Freeman starts away from the Saleen, following the old man.

Jack takes a final look at the car: Other than the cracked driver's window, the missing windshield, and the gaping holes in the door and the roof, it looks perfectly intact, near mint, from a ways away.

Not that that's saying much; it's still a retro-craze, wannabe throwback made out of tin foil.

11

Nordstrom's is at the center of the mall next to the two-level parking garage where O'Malley was found in his car. Jack smiles at the first thing he sees: a painting crew outside the department store.

Freeman crosses the front of the store and pulls up next to the curb closest to the crew's scaffold. The painters are starting to set up for their night's work, pouring paint into trays and mounting new rollers onto long handles.

Freeman asks, "How we play this?"

"We walk up. You be muscle; I'll be mouth. Take it slow. See how they respond."

"Fair enough." Freeman opens his door, and Jack feels the car rise as the shocks rebound from the displaced weight. Before Jack can get out, he hears one of the painters whistle.

"Whoo! Look who we have here!"

As Jack stands up, he sees the guy closest to them put his hand on his hip and give Freeman the twice-over. He has his cap on backward and the same white, paint-spattered clothes that most painters wear, but with a short taffeta scarf around his neck.

"You all see what I'm seeing?" He looks up at the other painter, but the guy is staring at Freeman. When Taffeta turns back to Freeman, he gets the same message his friend got: Freeman doesn't like the attention.

On the second level of the scaffold, not ten feet above Jack, the other painter whispers something to Taffeta. Jack can't hear anything except for the letters NFL.

"That's right, boys. This here is Freeman Jones from the New York Jets, J-E-T-S. Formerly a five-time Pro Bowl selection." Jack smiles at the painters, his hands extended like the ringmaster in a one-ring circus.

"Sergeant Haggerty?" the guy on the scaffold says. This guy's inked up like he put his own art on with a roller, his neck covered to his chin.

Jack laughs; it's been a long time since someone has confused him and Mike Haggerty.

"That's Jack Palms. Hey, what's up, Jack?" Taffeta comes toward Jack with his hand out, takes Jack's, and launches into a multistage handshake that moves from one grip to another without any signal as to what comes next. Jack lets his hand go limp and, like a bad dance partner, lets the guy lead him along.

Taffeta ends his hand dance with a quick one-armed embrace.

"Yeah," Tattoos says. "That's what I mean. Sergeant Haggerty from *Shake Me Down*. But serious, what the fuck happened to your hair?"

"We just had a few questions. Like if you were here the night before last?"

"Ha. Questions? I got one for you: How the parties at those LA hot spots, Jack dear?" Taffeta holds the back of his hand to his mouth, covering a big smile. "I seen you in the papers too.

Broke up with your wife. Before you grew this terrible hairdo."

Freeman steps forward, and Taffeta goes quiet.

"Questions," Jack says.

Tattoos nods. "We were here. We found the car with the dead cop in it. Saw the shit you heard about on the news."

"This all of you?" Jack gestures to the two, a small crew for a store as big as Nordstrom's.

"Bob's still in the truck."

Jack looks over and sees a third painter standing by their van, smoking a cigarette. He tilts his chin up at Jack, takes a hard pull off the cigarette, and tosses it out onto the sidewalk.

Jack says, "Tell me what you saw."

Tattoos drops down from the scaffold. "It was bad, like you probably heard. But there was a girl too. Somehow she didn't make the papers."

"It's like we all told the cops, bro."

"Tell it again."

Taffeta asks, "Why you guys want to know? You're like an actor and a Jet. So why do you care?"

Freeman starts toward him and that ends that line of inquiry.

"Sure. No problem." Taffeta steps toward Jack. "We were painting this side of the building and saw a car come in late, like after four a.m. Too late to be anything good, but we figured it was probably some teenagers looking for a spot to fuck. New Mustang, so probably the head cheerleader, you know?"

"Anyway," Jack says.

The one called Bob comes up to where they're standing and leans against the scaffold. He looks tired, tired of painting, probably tired of it all. "We had to go down to the station. Spent all day with those dickheads at WCPD."

Tattoos points at him. "They did give us donuts, though. Just saying."

Freeman steps forward. He's getting impatient, but Jack doesn't know what to ask, how to get more out of them other than by feeling them out. "So you guys found the girl?" Jack says.

Taffeta says, "The girl, or the *woman*?"

"Well, we didn't find the woman." Bob smiles. "But we saw her. And *damn*, who could forget that, bro?"

"Smoking," Tattoos says. "She comes across the lot in her skirt suit, pretty as you can imagine, like she's just walking into the office. Four-thirty in the morning, and she gets into your boy's yellow Mustang."

"So then I knew it wasn't a couple of high schoolers."

"She gets done, she drives off. Walks back to her car, don't even peel out."

"Bro, and that's *after* the gunshots, keep in mind."

Jack wishes he was writing this down. "Who was she? What'd she look like?"

Taffeta says, "Like he said, she was stunning. Blond, stylish, very *adult*."

"Huh?" Tattoos and Bob look at Taffeta as if they got a whiff of bad paint.

"What was she driving?"

"Car was mint. A dark pimp sedan with all-tint windows."

"Like the kind you slow down for on the highway. Undercover shit."

"*Really?*" Jack asks. He looks at Freeman.

Bob raises his eyebrows. "You know those cars when you see

them. And she had a briefcase."

"A Crown Vic," Tattoos says. "But I didn't see no briefcase."

Taffeta holds up his hand like he's being sworn in. "Sure as I'm standing here, I saw her briefcase."

Bob and Tattoos look at Taffeta, and finally Tattoos shrugs. "I didn't get that good a look."

"Anyway," Jack says, "briefcase or not, did she come on the scene before or after you heard the shots?"

"Before," Bob says. "She was most definitely here when it all went down."

"And you all agree it was two shots?"

They nod. Jack looks at Freeman, who shifts his eyes toward the car. He takes a step in its direction, down off the curb.

"Right. Anything else you can remember? Something we should know that you didn't tell the cops?"

"Who are you guys? Why you even give a shit?"

Freeman cracks his knuckles. "Let's just say we do."

"Okay. Okay." Bob holds his hands up. "Scene in the backseat with the girl was nasty. Almost made me not come to work today." He shakes his head.

Taffeta says, "I couldn't even tell my wife about it." Bob and Tattoos look away.

Freeman cocks his head toward the car again.

"Thanks," Jack tells the guys. He holds up his hand.

"One of the shots was fucking loud," Tattoos says in a monotone. "Louder than the first one."

"The loud one was first, bro," Bob says.

Taffeta and Tattoos both stop for a beat. "Yeah," they both say.

Bob goes on: "The loud one came first. Definitely."

"Loud?" Jack asks. "How do you mean?"

"Like a cannon," Freeman says. "The fifty."

Bob nods. "First one was like, *boom!* I mean that shit could've been a fucking truck exploding. It got your attention."

"Yeah," Tattoos says. "That's why I was sure the second one was a gunshot. I stopped dead after that. Like what the fuck?"

"You tell that to the police?"

"No," Bob says. He hops up onto the bottom part of the scaffold.

"Why not?"

"Because they didn't ask, bro."

Freeman says softly, "Or because they already knew."

"Alright," Jack says. "Two shots, guys. Thanks for the info."

"When's the Haggerty sequel coming out, Jack?" Tattoos asks.

Taffeta pulls his scarf a little tighter. "And how about those parties in LA? Tell us what they're like."

"Got to go," Jack says.

Freeman's already getting into the car.

12

"Bunch of fucking losers," Freeman says, driving across the lot. "Didn't tell us shit."

"How about that woman they saw walking away? Who was she?"

Freeman tilts his big head. "Yeah—"

"Hold up. I want to see the spot where O'Malley was parked."

Freeman stops the car and looks at Jack, looks at him hard.

"Let's check out the second level of the garage." Jack waves toward the two-story parking structure.

"The fuck, Jack? You think this is what a real detective would do?"

Jack looks across the car at Freeman wedged behind the steering wheel with the seat way back and reclining. "What would a real detective do?"

"A real detective would sit at home and scour the Internet first, find out whatever he could about his dead guy, *everything*, and then he'd find out more. He'd poke around with the living people who knew the guy, people who can tell him something good. Those fucks?" He nods his head toward the painting crew. "They couldn't tell you shit you won't find in today's paper. Maybe tomorrow's."

Jack thinks it over. "I guess I'm more of a hands-on guy. You know, follow the clues that I come to."

"Did you read the newspapers today, all of them? And get everything you could out of your boy on the force, the guy who brought you into this?"

Jack thinks about what Sergeant Mike Haggerty would have said at a time like this, what he would do about finding O'Malley's killer. In *Shake 'Em Down*, Haggerty would have gotten attacked by the painters, who turned out to be secret agents for the mob, beaten them down, and then wound up pursuing their leader in a high-speed car chase.

"You there, Jack? What's going on in your head?"

"I'm thinking about how I got my ass into this."

"That shit?" Freeman points at Jack's temple and shakes his head. "Thinking won't get you nowhere. You here now." He points to the floor of the car. "It don't matter how you got here, because you in it. You start second-guessing, it gets us both killed. I don't want to get shot at or worse. You hear?"

Jack nods.

"Now," Freeman says, but when he starts to say something, a look passes behind his eyes, a consideration of something else. Then it goes away. The big man puts the car into drive and heads into the parking structure. He follows the ramp up to the second level, where the Saleen was parked.

"What would that slug do after it went through O'Malley's car? Would it leave a hole in the ground?"

"I want you to call your cop," Freeman says. "Find out what he knows and what he doesn't."

"We should also look for a building the sniper could've set up on."

"This ain't no *Dirty Harry*, Jack. You not going to find a slug—"

"But still." Jack gets out of the car and starts across the lot. It's late enough in the day now that whatever shoppers are still around have parked closer to the stores or downstairs. The upper level, more of an overflow lot than anything else, sits almost empty.

He can see the painting crew about fifty yards off and the progress they've made on the side of the Nordstrom's: about a third of the wall so far.

Freeman gets out of the car and warily looks around. Jack starts searching the ground, looking for something on the tarmac, he's not sure what.

"Shit," Freeman says.

And then Jack finds what he wanted: an angled ditch in the concrete big enough to stick his toes into, not more than three inches deep. He looks down into it and doesn't see anything; if there was something lodged here, it's gone now. Maybe the Walnut Creek police *aren't* doing such a bad job.

"Check this out," Jack says.

When Freeman comes over, he whistles. "Good shit." He crouches down and puts his fingers into the hole. From the way his arm points out of it, if the bullet went through the car roof to door, O'Malley wasn't parked within the white lines. But at that hour he probably didn't care. He'd have just pulled onto the lot, angled however he wanted. Jack looks up and sees the one building the sniper could have been on top of: a restaurant a hundred yards away with a big bing crosby's sign on the roof.

"Right about there," Jack says, pointing.

"Yeah." Freeman stands up, and they both stay where they are, facing the restaurant, looking at its roof.

"Hard to imagine putting a shot through a guy's car from that far out, knowing it'd take his head off."

"You'd be surprised what these guns can do, Jack. Some sick shit."

"So who the fuck was that woman?"

Freeman shakes his head. "I'm saying it's time you called your friend the cop. See what more he can tell us."

Jack's got the phone in his hand and is speed-dialing Hopkins's number before Freeman can finish the thought.

Hopkins picks up on the third ring.

"I got some questions for you, Mills."

"You better get your ass down here to the Embarcadero, Jack. We just found something you're not going to like. Another girl's been killed. Looks like the same MO as the girl in O'Malley's car."

13

As the Mercedes comes out of the Caldecott Tunnel through the Oakland hills, headed toward the Bay, Freeman grunts and starts shaking his head. He carefully slides his hand underneath his long hair, then cradles the back of his neck in his palm and massages. Jack sees another tattoo at the top of his shoulder coming out of his shirt. He turns to look through the windshield, waiting for the familiar San Francisco skyline. The two of them have been quiet for more than fifteen minutes, and Jack knows the big Samoan will talk when he's ready.

"What's up with the girl, Jack? You know how a girl like that ends up in this city? What type of shit she gets into?"

Jack shakes his head.

"Slavery. Buying and selling of people. Here in SF. You spend enough time in North Beach like I've been and you know."

"Unh-unh."

"Ownership, Jack. That, plus someone with power in the city is protecting it. You sure you ready for that?"

Jack watches the trees, thinks back to being on the road with the Czechs and the rush of feeling as if his life were in his hands. The bike put him out there on the edge, something he never felt when he was trying to get himself clean, reading and hitting the gym. Back then it was more about what he didn't do than what he did.

"Yeah," he says. "I want to know what happened and how she ended up where she did. I want to know who sent O'Malley after me."

"These motherfuckers don't play, Jack. You see how they killed her?"

"They slit her throat. I saw the pictures." As they come out of the hills, Jack can see the lights of downtown Oakland, and beyond that, the Bay Bridge.

"If someone put down big cash on this girl, that person be pissed when she's dead. Akakievich don't have penny-ante clients. It could mean he's ready to take issue with a big player. And now there's a second girl?" Freeman shakes his head and whistles. "That could mean he's going after something big, like he wants something. I'm starting to wonder if I shouldn't just drop your ass off downtown and opt out of this shit."

"What?" Jack turns to Freeman, tries to read his face. "Now you're the one who's thinking too much. Are you serious?"

"This is big."

Jack takes out his cigarettes. Freeman's eyes dart toward Jack's hands, and he's already lowering the window before Jack has one out of the pack. "You smoke, that window comes down."

Jack lights up. The first drag slows him down and gives him a new outlook on what he sees through the windshield: They're not just heading into the city, they're plowing straight into a world of trouble.

14

When they get to the Embarcadero, Jack calls Hopkins from the coffee shop like he's supposed to. He orders an espresso and downs it, heads outside to wait. Caffeine is Jack's rush now—not like the woozy down from alcohol or the incredible highs he got from the Colombian marching powder. It's caffeine, a cigarette to smooth it out, and Jack's in the life. That's his high.

After a few minutes, Hopkins rounds the corner, still wearing the same old-fashioned Panama hat he probably thinks makes him look like a real cop. That or he's old enough to be from the school where people actually wore them. Jack comes around to the idea of the second, ditches his cigarette when Hopkins gets close.

"Where the fuck you been? I've been waiting to show you the scene already."

Freeman stands up to his full height from leaning against the car and gives Hopkins a hard stare.

"Who the fuck is this?" Hopkins points his chin at the big Samoan.

"This is my backup," Jack says. "He's on your payroll too."

"That's great. I get the fucking USA All Stars: an actor and a New York Jet. That'll keep you two low profile."

Jack starts to say something, but Hopkins beats him to it. "Come on. Fuck it." He points at Freeman. "And you stay here."

Freeman waves it off with an "I'm good," and heads around the back of the car to wait inside. Judging by the look on his face, he's happier the farther he stays from the cops.

As they head up the block, Hopkins takes off his hat and hands it to Jack. "Wear this. The fewer people who recognize you, the better."

"I've got a couple of questions about the shooting. Did you know someone put a fifty-caliber slug through that car?"

"No, but that sure explains what happened to O'Malley's head." Hopkins points toward the next perpendicular street, and they make a turn around the corner. When they do, Jack sees twin light towers illuminating the scene of the police investigation: the yellow tape, a few onlookers, the whole nine yards. In the middle of it all is a maroon four-door Chevy.

"I saw the Mustang in impound. It has a hole in the roof you can put your arm through. Same for the door."

Hopkins takes his eyes off their destination for a second to check Jack's look, and Jack puts on the hat, pulls it down over his eyebrows. Hopkins holds up the yellow tape for him to enter. "I hear you, Jack. But I think what I'm about to show you is worse."

He holds up his badge to the first cop in dress uniform he sees and says "Forensics—he's our blood spatter expert" when the guy points his head at Jack.

Hopkins directs Jack toward the car. "We got a call about two hours ago. Somebody sees a girl inside a parked car, she's not moving, doesn't have clothes on, doesn't look good. We get down here and find this. Now these guys are checking the car for prints. Least we'll get to investigate this one, I hope."

"Where's the girl?"

"Come on." Hopkins walks toward a big dark-blue police truck. In the back of the truck, a gurney supports a body covered by a blanket. Hopkins climbs in and motions for Jack to follow. Inside, he lifts the blanket off the girl's head. She's as young as the first girl, blond where the first was brunette but with skin just as white, like she never spent a day in the sun. She's practically translucent, glowing.

Her blond hair falls around her face thick with dark red blood. The blood looks like it ran up from her neck, over her face, and into her hair, where it's dried in clumps though some of it still looks wet. She's clean from the neck down, except a few dark bruises around her shoulders. Her neck is the most shocking: gaping open, as if someone had tried to cut her head off with a saw.

"Back of that car was clean. Wherever she lost most of her eight pints, it wasn't there."

"Shit," Jack says. "Any idea who she is?"

"Huh-unh. We're trying to see if we can link her to the girl they found in Walnut Creek, the one in O'Malley's backseat."

"Fucking sixteen-year-old girls?"

Hopkins shakes his head, scratches his chin. "You don't have to tell me shit about it, Jack. I got a daughter myself coming up on about this age."

"This one cuffed?"

"Same. Left like the first. But no marks on her legs."

Jack steps away from the girl's body. "What's happening?"

70

"Shit, Jack. You tell me someone shot a hole through a cop's car with something like an antitank gun, and I got two dead girls in two days. Who's got answers?"

Jack blinks. When he closes his eyes, he can still see the girl, the blood caked around her face and thick in her hair, trails of it running up her cheeks. Her shoulders look like they could fit into a young boy's clothes. Her thin lips are already turning white.

"Freeman says it's a message."

"What?"

"That these girls are somebody's message. There's a slave trade for sex and if you own this girl, it's somebody telling you to be ready."

"Ready for what? More killing?"

Jack follows Hopkins out of the truck now. Back down on the street, Hopkins waits, staring at him for an answer.

"I don't know. Something bad."

"Does this mean terrorism?"

"I don't know." Jack shrugs. "These girls go to people with power and money. If someone's pulling the plug on their fun, it's not going to sit well."

Hopkins spits on the ground. "I found out more about O'Malley: They had him stationed in North Beach, watching a porn-and-prostitution ring. Word is it had links to the Russian mob and some high-level shit, also that he asked for the job specifically."

Jack's about to tell Hopkins about Alexi Akakievich's goons in the alley when he sees an attractive blond in a gray business suit on the other side of the crime scene. She's talking to a couple of guys in dark suits. "Who the fuck is that?" Jack asks. He nods at the threesome and Hopkins turns to look, but as soon as he does, he spins, grabs Jack by the arm, and ushers him toward the Chevy.

He speaks softly, close to Jack's ear. "That's the Feds. They see you in here and I'm entirely fucked."

"What are they—"

"Fuck." Hopkins spits out the word with a jerk of his neck. "I'm fucked anyway. They show up here, they're probably going to take this one too."

"Too?"

"Word I got about O'Malley's stakeout is it got taken over last week. Taken away from him by the Feds."

Jack ducks behind Hopkins to get another look at the blond. She's intent on her conversation with the two men, looks like she's getting upset.

"I interviewed the painters who found O'Malley's body. They said they saw a blond who looked just like your Fed friend walking away from the scene after they heard the shooting."

"Shit." Now Hopkins takes a quick look over.

Jack checks out the car. A few fingerprint guys move around, dusting the car's handles with little brushes.

"Whose car is this?"

"Stolen." Hopkins shakes his head. "Gives us nothing."

"Let's go over and ask the Fed if she was at the scene of O'Malley's murder. Ask *her* what she saw."

Jack starts to move, but Hopkins catches his arm above the elbow. "Can't do that, Jack. That would be a very big mistake." He leads Jack away from the Chevy toward the yellow police tape on the side of the scene opposite from the Feds.

"Why not? If she knows something, then we should go find out, right?"

Hopkins squeezes Jack's arm tighter, bumps him as they walk. One of the blue uniforms sees this and looks at them funny, but then turns away quickly when he sees Hopkins's gold badge.

"Just shut up, Jack. Shut the fuck up."

When they're outside the yellow tape, Hopkins lets go of Jack's arm. He leads them back toward the Mercedes. "You don't want to mix with the Feds," he says. "Do I need to tell you how fucked we are if the Feds are involved in this city's corruption."

"But I—"

"No. Fuck that. It's no shocker if some of my compatriots are taking payouts and stand knee-deep in shit with a guy like Akakievich, but if the Feds are tied up in it too, then we're talking about a mess on a national level, something neither of us gets to walk away from."

They both stop. They stare back up the street at the bright lights of the crime scene. One of the Feds is talking to a cop on the perimeter, pointing back in the direction of the car. The blond stands beside him, gesturing toward the truck where the girl is.

"We got to back off on this for a minute, Jack. I need to talk to someone who might know what all we're getting into."

"Who's that?"

15

After Freeman's dropped him off at his hotel, Jack can't sleep.

He finds himself sitting at the desk in his room at 2:14 a.m., smoking and staring out the window at the lights of Union Square.

He's still unsure what it'll take to make his house safe territory again, what he can do about staying somewhere permanently if it's not safe. For now he's happy to be in the hotel, away from where he can be found, but he knows this can only go on so long, that sooner or later someone will find him or Hopkins will find out how much this is costing.

His gaze turns to the bright Macy's across the square, its gleaming lights. In a couple of months, Christmas will come and the square will be decorated like this but way more. Brighter, louder, with more energy. And maybe people in the hotel will still sit up at two-thirty in the morning, making plans for the next day.

Jack imagines the strip bars over in North Beach going full swing on this Friday night, girls dancing at the Pretty Lady and Larry Flint's, maybe going home with guys or taking them into dimly lit back rooms for handjobs and more. He shakes his head and crosses the room to the dresser, starts to pull on his jeans.

Downstairs Jack hails a taxi, knowing he'd be better off with Freeman, but he's determined to get what new information he can find tonight. Fuck sleeping or waiting; there's enough going on out there to keep him busy.

As his taxi heads north, he thinks back to the incident in the alley and the way it might have ended for him without Freeman. Now he'll be more careful. Now he knows. He wears his old Red Sox baseball hat pulled down, glad for the anonymity it offers.

Out the taxi window, he sees the same streets he saw when he came looking for Freeman. Soon he sees people walking the streets in club clothes—lots of leather jackets and women in tight black pants or short skirts. He sees the nightclubs and bars, closed now, leaving only the action of the late-night strip clubs, which is exactly how Jack wants it. He has the cabbie turn onto Broadway, heading toward the Bay. They pass by Freeman's club, and Jack says to stop and let him out.

In front of the Pretty Lady, the same two big guys in suits stand ready to bounce, ready to start kicking people out when the place closes at four.

Jack walks up to the two guys, nods.

"No hats inside, pal. We have a dress code."

Jack looks at the bouncer, holds up his hands. "I'm a friend of Freeman's. You remember me from before?"

"Right. Right. Shit, yeah. We saw you with him the other night. He says you Jack Palms from the movies."

"I owed Big Free some money off an old bet and when I gave it to him, he said he was going to find some nice ass."

The guys laugh. One elbows the other and shakes his head. "Fucking Freeman."

"The guy never touches a girl the whole time he's here, doesn't tell us nothing, then you come along and he's popping his cherry. What a fuck."

Jack laughs. "Yeah. He said he'd heard about a place he had to try, kind of deal where he could get a nice lily-white girl, high gloss. Said he'd never had the right kind of money to blow on that tail before." Jack acts the part, shrugs off that this might seem a strange thing for Freeman to do. "You know where I can find some of that?"

The second guy nods. "You mean Top Notch. Place is the fucking speakeasy Holy Grail right now. The most secret. But Free ain't getting in there, hear?"

The two laugh, slap hands.

Jack smiles. "Yeah. Exactly. I just came into some cash myself, you know?" He raises his eyebrows.

"Right." The big suit hits Jack in the arm. "Yeah. They exclusive, but for a guy from the movies, they'll be sure and let you in. Just don't be yapping about it." He pauses, squinting at Jack. "So what was you in?"

"You're an idiot," the other bouncer says, and turns away to pat down a couple of businessmen looking to go inside.

Jack shakes the guy's hand. "I'm Jack Palms. I was in—"

"Ha! Yeah! *Shake That Around.*"

"Exactly."

When the other bouncer turns back, he nods and points at Jack. "Right. Sorry about this dumbass, Jack." He hits his friend across the chest. "*Shake 'Em Down.* 1999."

"That's cool."

"But you know it was bullshit you'd kill that many guys in

the movie." He catches Jack's arm at the bicep, gives it a squeeze. "No fucking way. I'd believe that shit from Bruce Lee, Jackie Chan or Jet Li, some martial arts master, even Steven fucking Segal. But not some regular dude." He shakes his head. "No, not you."

"Yeah, you got a point, bro." Now the other bouncer scrutinizes Jack. "Yeah. I mean fun movie, but if you were expected to believe it? Forget that shit. Who the fuck *are* you?"

Jack smiles, holds up his hands. "I don't write 'em, boys, just act 'em." He shrugs. "They tell me where to stand, who to kick and punch, I say the lines, right?"

"And get paid!" They both laugh and give each other high fives. "Yeah, man. Let me know when you're doing a sequel and I'll really make it believable. I'll fucking tear through some guys." He opens his hand and turns the movement into a big hand-shaking affair.

"No sequel plans yet," Jack says, his hand cupped inside the bouncer's palm. "Maybe they agree with you about me being a regular guy. But if it changes, I'll let you know."

"No. I mean it." The guy pulls a card out of his jacket, hands it to Jack. "You call me up. I *definitely* want to get in on that Hollywood bank."

Jack gives the card a quick look and pockets it. "You were going to tell me how I get to the Top Notch?"

"Yeah. Yeah. Top Notch. They run that shit out of the back of Tedeschi's Café. It's three streets up. You go left on Bartol." The bouncer points farther up the hill. "Ask for dessert, you know what I'm saying? That's the hookup."

16

At Bartol, really more of a glorified alley than a street, Jack can see the small café—a storefront with a couple of tables and a naked light bulb. It's a good front; you'd never believe this little late-night coffee-and-dessert spot off the beaten path would be selling access to women.

If the other bouncers thought Freeman could find the place on his own, then why didn't the big man say something to Jack earlier? And what else is he holding back?

Then Jack gets his answer. He sees Freeman start down Bartol coming from the other direction, walking toward Tedeschi's, his head down and his eyes intent on where he's headed. Jack ducks into a doorway and watches. Freeman nods at a guy smoking a cigarette at a sidewalk table out front of the café, then walks by him and heads inside.

"The fuck?" Jack says under his breath. He feels as though he's just been jabbed in the gut.

What else can he do? He moves slowly up the alley to get a better view of the café, making sure the guy at the table isn't watching. Inside, Freeman's wide body blocks his transaction at the counter, but then he turns around, holding some kind of dessert—maybe tiramisu?—on a little plate and sits down. He forks a few spoonfuls into his mouth and then gets up, dumps the rest in the trash, and puts the plate in a gray plastic bin on top of the trash can. Then he looks at his receipt, a small rectangle of white paper, pockets it, and walks out.

Jack ducks into a dark doorway. He hears Freeman bark something at the smoker, a guy Jack thinks is a little too slick to be hanging out by himself at a late-night café. He's got gelled-back hair and wears a thick shearling coat, the fuzzy white collar standing up around his face. He reminds Jack of someone he's seen before, or maybe he just looks too much like the standard bouncer.

When Jack looks again, Freeman's walking away, back up the alley in the direction he came. Jack lets him get ten yards farther on before he starts to follow. At the next street, Vallejo, Freeman makes a right. Then, less than a block later, he turns right again. Jack walks up Vallejo, listening for steps or someone breathing before he turns the corner. If Freeman's made him, he doesn't want to walk into the big man's fist. He doesn't want to walk into the big man's *anything*.

But when he finally peers around the corner, into a dark, even thinner alley than Bartol—a sign reads prescott court—what Jack sees is a short dead end, not even a full block. About halfway down, Freeman walks up the stairs to a house, knocks, and then holds up his receipt and says something. Jack can make out the loud click of a lock opening, and then Freeman steps inside. The door closes.

"Fuck me." Now Jack knows he's lost a friend.

He pulls out his pack and mouths a cigarette between his lips, lights it. Trying to look as nonchalant as possible, he walks down the right side of the narrow alley, staying opposite the door Freeman went into. There are no houses on this side, nothing more than a few doors, places that probably have a main entrance somewhere else. At the end it's a Dumpster and another building and a thin walkway that probably leads out to another street.

Jack makes to look at the windows—just a friendly guy out for a night stroll on a dark dead end—and then glances over at the door Freeman went into. He can't tell if he's being watched; the windows on the front of the house are all black. At the end of the alley, he turns around, looks up at the windows on his right. He wonders if O'Malley was ever on a stakeout in one of them, or if he'd been working for the Russians in the house the whole time.

Jack wonders if there's a stakeout going on now. Maybe the blond Fed is watching from one of these houses. Shit, Jack thinks, she could be inside the house Freeman just went into.

As Jack heads toward Vallejo, he looks back to see if he can see a number on the door Freeman went into. There's a small sign: 32 prescott court. With luck, Hopkins will have something on that address to give Jack tomorrow.

17

Jack thinks about knocking on the door to 32 Prescott Court but knows that's not the best idea. Especially with Freeman around. He can't resist going back to Tedeschi's, though, to see what's what with the desserts, to check out the operation.

Jack drops the butt of his cigarette onto the sidewalk, crushes it out with his shoe.

He backtracks and turns toward the café, heading right for the man at the table outside. The guy's finished his smoke and is leaning back, a cup of coffee on the table and a newspaper with foreign block lettering in front of his face. When Jack gets to within ten feet, the guy looks up over the top of the paper. Jack's still in the street, not even on the sidewalk yet, and the guy lowers the paper enough to see above it, cutting his face off at the bridge of his nose. His eyes narrow a bit; he takes in Jack's jeans and the too-worn leather jacket, and he nods, goes back to reading.

Jack nods back and says "Hey" to the guy as he walks through the doors and into the café. At one of the tables, a pair of twenty-somethings scarf cake and ice cream, drinking fancy coffee out of clear glass cups. A pair of stubble-faced old men sit at the other table, playing a card game. Jack walks to the counter and looks at some fancy cakes, a few flavors of gelato, tiramisu, and what he hopes is a plastic version of *île flottante*. He orders the tiramisu from a black-haired counter girl. She's hot, but not bust-out-of-your-mind hot, big up top and wearing tight jeans that don't hide much. With a lot of eyeliner on, she's about what you'd expect at an all-night café.

After Jack orders, the girl takes a plated tiramisu out of the refrigerated case. Then, at the register, she stops for a second, looking past him. In the mirror behind her, Jack sees the guy shake his head, a slight turn of his chin. She asks Jack if he wants anything else, and when he says no, rings up his charge for $3.50.

Jack pays, takes his receipt and a fork, and sits down at a counter by the window. He tries the tiramisu: not the best he's ever had, but pretty good. Nothing special. The receipt is a plain register printout: faint numbering, the time, the charge, the tax, his total. Nothing special. On the other side of the window, the guy's back to reading his newspaper, a new cigarette lit and resting on the edge of an ashtray beside his coffee.

Jack takes another bite of the tiramisu and stands up. The guy outside lowers his paper. He's looking up the alley toward Vallejo, but for all Jack knows, he's waiting for Jack's next move. He dumps the rest of his dessert and puts his plate in the plastic bin as Freeman had done earlier. He looks back at the girl. She smiles, but not too genuinely; she looks like she'll be happy to see Jack gone. He checks his receipt again, pockets it, and walks out.

Outside, Jack tries to catch the smoker's eye but gets nothing, not even a glance. For the briefest of moments, Jack rocks back on his heels, thinks of stopping and saying something, but then he doesn't. He puts his weight on his toes and keeps walking, makes a right and goes back toward Broadway, away from Vallejo, Prescott Court, and Freeman Jones.

It's time to be careful, to stay far away from anything that might get him hurt.

The way things look, he might as well hail a cab and make for the hotel.

He looks at his watch: It's coming up on four a.m. Where the hell else is he going to go?

Part II

The Guy Who Came in from the Cold

18

Too early the next morning, Jack hears his cell phone buzzing and ringing at the same time, a feature it's adopted without knowing how or why—or how to stop it. By the time he gets his eyes open, he hears the beep of a message hitting his voicemail. He pulls himself up to look around, sees daylight outside the window, then the clock—8:07—and swears. Finally he picks up his phone. The missed call is from Mills Hopkins.

Jack holds the phone in front of him, stares at it, trying to get his brain started. He's got some big questions for Sergeant Hopkins and a potential problem with his huge wingman. It doesn't take him more than a second to remember that.

But for Hopkins to call him early like this has to mean there's something new he's going to have to handle. He calls his voicemail and cradles the phone between his ear and shoulder, takes a cigarette off the nightstand—a nasty habit, especially at this hour of the morning—and thinks about breaking the rules again.

Hopkins's message is brief. He's got information to discuss, something that can't wait, and he wants Jack to meet him by the Embarcadero Center.

"Get your ass down here, Palms" is the last line of the

message, "and we'll talk when you do."

A half hour later, showered and with an egg-and-cheese sandwich in his gut, Jack stands on a sidewalk along Davis Street. Even this early on a Saturday, the tourists and shoppers are out in full force.

Jack calls Hopkins from a phone booth using his cell phone, not wanting to sit out in the open, and the old cop answers while walking the beat on his day off, looking around the area where they found the second girl to see if he can turn up anything else. Good cop Hopkins can't even take a morning off to settle in and calm himself down, Jack thinks. The fuck will probably keep walking beats even after he's retired, trying to solve crimes for free.

They agree to meet near where Jack is, at a small patch of grass and a piece of hill with some trees. Not something you'd even call a park.

Jack walks up the block and around a corner, gets there before Hopkins, so he sits on a bench and lights up. He takes a look around, trying to get his bearings.

It's a sunny morning in late fall, probably the sunniest time of year in the city, with less fog than the summer months and even some truly warm days. Today's not warm, though, and Jack's got on the motorcycle jacket he still means to get rid of. He can see the wide thoroughfare of the Embarcadero and off to his right a broad, open courtyard with a huge modern sculpture and a barricaded area where they'll set up an ice rink soon.

Tall, thin trees whistle in the breeze. About twenty feet up, branches and leaves sprout from the white trunks, and Jack can see birds: colorful green birds that can't possibly be pigeons. He turns and looks up to see better. Not only are the birds too colorful to be pigeons—Jack sees a lot of bright green and even some yellow—but there are far too many of them. Like a friendlier version of Alfred Hitchcock's *The Birds*.

"Those are the parrots," Hopkins says. He's behind Jack suddenly, coming up from a path Jack hadn't noticed.

Jack pops up. "Fuck, Mills. You're killing me."

"Those cigarettes, *those* are killing you." Hopkins takes his hands out of his pockets and sits down on the bench. "Those aren't the parrots from the movie, mind you, but they're our parrots, the pride of the city or something like that."

"Nice," Jack says. The birds have large beaks, more colors on their bodies than Jack can make out. "They're chirping like it's Christmas."

"Yeah. People think they just talk about crackers or pirate bullshit. But that's not true. Obviously."

Jack doesn't sit back down. He asks Hopkins what's up and takes a long drag off his cigarette.

Hopkins shakes his head. His eyes have focused on something far away.

"Got nothing on the big gun from Walnut Creek," he says, shrugs. "They're keeping mum about it. As for who would own a gun like that, it's anybody's guess. As illegal as they're supposed to be, I've heard of local drug runners in the East Bay having them. I mean small-time *punks*."

"I'm worried about Freeman." Now Jack sits down. "I think he's gone over. Switched sides on me."

"Shit." Hopkins turns to Jack and asks why, so Jack explains about seeing him on Bartol and following him back to Prescott

Court. When he gets to that detail, Hopkins nods.

"Yeah," he says. "Prescott Court is where O'Malley was spending his time. I still can't get much info, but that name has come up. There's shit going down."

Jack looks away. He drops his cigarette butt onto the ground and crushes it with his shoe. "In any case, it looks like I'm on my own now. It has me more than a little worried."

"Stick with Freeman then. Watch him, let him watch you. But don't let him know you saw him cross. Could be he leads you to something we can use."

"Could be he leads me to getting my ass killed!" Jack stands, and a number of parrots shift from one tree to another in a flutter and beating of wings. "Tell me something good. What you got?"

Hopkins slips his wallet out of his jacket's inside pocket and takes out a card. He hands it to Jack. "This is the guy you can trust. He's my connection at Walnut Creek, and he's ready to help."

The card features the crest of the Walnut Creek PD and the name Alvin Shaw.

"His cell's on the back. Anything you need, bring him in. Guy's a whole different breed of cop."

"Is that good?"

"It *is* good. For you."

"What's he doing in Walnut Creek?"

"What can he do? His wife made him move to the suburbs. But he's the goods. Former military, the kind people don't talk about: some heavy black ops shit those Walnut Creek cops don't understand. They'll never understand most things about this guy."

"Yeah?"

"Trust me," Hopkins says. "Trust him. He knows how you've been working for me."

Above them, the parrots' wings beat loud and fast all of a sudden, and then the whole pack of them, what looks like fifty birds, flies out of the trees and away. A mass of dark green bodies moves east toward the Bay and then turns toward downtown.

Hopkins stands up, holding onto his hat. For a moment, the sound of the wings flapping is all Jack can hear. But then a new sound wipes that clean away: A boom fills the morning air, reverberates off the tall buildings, loud, more like a cannon than anything Jack's ever heard. It leaves everything quiet in its wake.

19

Jack starts and falls back. He sees Hopkins fly through the air as if a giant arm had punched him into the trees more than five feet from where he'd been standing a moment before. Jack steps toward him and stops: There's more blood on the ground already than he can imagine. Hopkins grabs at his shoulder with a blood-wet hand, clutching at himself with fingers that seem to move of their own accord as his eyes blink open and shut.

"Oh, fuck me," Hopkins wheezes. He tries to roll over onto his side, and when he does, a new sound comes out of him, a gurgle, and a stream of blood coughs its way out of his mouth.

Hopkins shakes his head, looks at Jack with wide eyes over what's left of his shoulder, pieces of collar bone and torn muscle hanging open for all the world to see.

"You're going to be all right," Jack says, knowing it isn't true.

"Fuck." Hopkins spits out a gob of phlegm and blood. "Go. Run."

Jack looks around, crouches as he turns and gets behind the bench, then looks in the direction where the shot must have come from. He sees nothing. Slowly he backs toward Hopkins, watching the buildings for any movement, and suddenly he sees a flash, hears the sound of an explosion.

Jack drops onto his chest and looks up to see a big chunk blown out of a tree not three feet away. Something hit the tree about chest height, in its thickest part, and it still took away almost half its width. With a creaking, cracking sound, the tree starts to lean, then fall. It gets caught in the branches of another tree and stops. Jack looks at Hopkins and sees there's now a trickle of white foam coming from his mouth. But he's still breathing, shaking his head in small jerky movements as if he might be going into shock.

Jack stands and, as fast as he can, jukes and twists away from the bench, a motion he hopes a sniper wouldn't predict. Another shot tears the air around him, then a scream from somewhere close, and Jack realizes he's not in a world by himself. There are other people around him: other potential victims, other witnesses.

He runs, head tucked and changing directions, goes for the tall wooden boards that will soon house the ice rink. If he can get to the other side—

Another shot. Jack sees a hole punched into the boards a few feet in front of him and cuts to his left, but his foot slips on the wet tiles of the courtyard. He goes down hard, hitting his chin on the cement, rolls, keeps his momentum, and scrambles up into a running crawl, his hands still hitting the ground as he pushes forward the last few feet toward protection. He stops. Prone, with his head down, he waits, breathing hard against the ground, his lungs burning.

He runs his tongue along his teeth, making sure none of them broke when he hit his chin. His tongue is still there, but he tastes blood.

He listens.

From not too far away, he hears a scream and then a man yelling in a Slavic language. Two car doors slam. Someone honks twice, angrily, and yells a few choice four-letter words.

Beyond the trees, an older man hides behind the large black-and-white sculpture that's been there for as long as Jack can remember. Near him, a woman in a short black skirt covers her ears with her hands.

Jack hears a sound like a car door slamming but different—perhaps a trunk. Then two more doors slam, and Jack moves a bit so he can see the street. A car picks up speed as it rounds a turn. It's a black sedan, American made, the kind you slow down for on the highway, thinking it's an unmarked.

Jack gets up slowly, still breathing hard. He scans the windows in the buildings for some sign of the sniper, the big gun. When he doesn't see anything, he's still not convinced he's safe.

20

After a few minutes of nothing, when the old man and the woman in the black skirt start to walk out from behind the sculpture and look around, Jack trots over to where he last saw Mills.

Hopkins isn't there.

His pool of blood covers a three-foot radius. His Panama lies on the ground, blown up against the trunk of a tree. Jack sees ragged marks of dirt along its side.

Jack swears. "Fuck" was the last word he heard from the cop. Even though he's woken himself in the middle of the night saying the word more times than he can count, spitting it out of a dream he can't remember, Jack knows this word shouldn't be Mills Hopkins's last. Hopkins deserves better. He's a good cop, a hard man who tried to do right.

A trail of crimson drops leads to the street, to where someone put him in the trunk of a Crown Victoria.

"Fuck," Jack says. "Fuck."

He doesn't know what to do now, standing in the park, the whole event spinning through his head, the few onlookers staring at him wide-eyed as though he's the one who just killed Mills.

"You okay, buddy?" someone asks.

Jack looks around.

A man takes two steps toward him and then stops when Jack looks his way.

"I want to help," the guy says. "Those dudes took your friend."

From somewhere in the distance, Jack hears the sound of a police cruiser.

He's sure of one thing: If the SFPD is as corrupt as Hopkins thought, he doesn't want to be caught at the scene of a cop shooting, the second for the SFPD in a few days.

Jack touches his pockets, realizes he's got the best lead he's going to get. He steps toward the street, away from the pool of blood on the ground and waves for a cab.

"Where you going, pal? I think you'd better stick around."

A cab stops, and Jack gets in, tells the driver to head toward Fisherman's Wharf, that he's going to the St. Francis but wants to take the long way. The safety of public places and crowds, then the quiet of his room for a little while so he can sort things out—that's what he needs. That and a gun.

Jack's eyes meet the eyes of the man who spoke to him, the guy who called him "pal." They stare at each other for a moment. The man's face is pure confusion, probably not so different from Jack's.

He turns away, looking out the window on the other side as the cab starts to gain speed. He watches runners scampering up the sidewalk, trying desperately to keep up with their lives.

This is the second friend Jack's seen gunned down in front of him, the third dead one since he left his house to work with Ralph and the Czechs. He closes his eyes, feels the rumble of the cab as its tires bump along the road.

Maybe he'd be better off running, never coming back to any of this. Get his Ducati and go. But he can't. Seeing Hopkins shot cemented that fact. Better to watch his step and see what he can find, tear down whatever walls need demolition, than to walk softly for the rest of his life, worrying that someone's close behind, lining him up in a set of crosshairs.

No. That's not for Jack. He'll choose life.

21

Jack gets out of the cab at the entrance to the bar in the St. Francis. The street outside is crowded, but a quick look inside the bar reveals it to be the quiet place Jack wants: a few couples talking, no ready-to-fight Russian suits, no hiding spots from where someone could line him up. The other patrons all appear to be tourists or people too old to be involved in the city's latest mess.

He walks up to the bar and stops in the middle, directly across from the mirror that reflects the view into the lobby. Jack looks up at the Talisker bottle perched high on its shelf. Then something in the mirror catches his eye, and when he looks at the reflection, his blood goes cold. Way across the lobby, on a wide tan couch near the far entrance to the hotel, Freeman sits flanked by two guys wearing dark suits.

The one on the right side has a bandage across his nose, right below two black eyes.

They're the same fucks from the alley, Black Suit and Gray Suit, the bad teeth brothers. Jack wonders if they talk to each other in the morning, make a collective decision about what color suit they should each wear. They probably share an apartment. Today they forgot to coordinate and both went with dark gray.

Jack looks right at Freeman, the friend he thought he could trust, and knows absolutely and completely that he is alone now. All he has is a "trustworthy" cop's business card and one chance to go upstairs and get the thing he never thought he'd have a use for: a gun.

The big man checks his watch. "Why you so nervous, Freeman?" Jack asks the reflection. "You got somewhere to be? Is someone waiting?"

"Can I help you, sir?" Jack hadn't seen the bartender coming, but now here he is, all starched white shirt, standing right in front of him.

Jack starts to say that he's fine, but then Freeman looks right at him, right through the bar's window and into the mirror, and their eyes meet. The big man squints.

"Shit," Jack says. He drops down below the mirror.

The bartender leans over, looks down at Jack. "You lose something?"

"No." Jack stays low and starts moving toward the bar's other door, the one that comes out by the elevators. The bartender watches as though he thinks Jack's a freak, but Jack has bigger issues to consider. As soon as he's past the window, he stands and makes his way into the bay of elevators.

Right as one's about to close, he jumps in. Behind him the doors shoot back open all the way. He catches a mean look from an older woman wearing some kind of brown fur hat. As the doors close all too slowly, Jack half expects to see Freeman's wide arm jut in between them. He counts his breaths, planning to grab Freeman's arm and break it back against the door.

Before the doors fully close, Jack sees Freeman pushing his way through the tourists.

Then the doors close and the car starts to rise. Jack slides to the back wall and tries to avoid making eye contact with any of the other riders. There are two white-haired women talking about something at the San Francisco Museum of Modern Art, and a mother and her teenage son standing in between bags from Macy's and a few of the other stores around Union Square. The boy's got his eye on an especially large bag from Niketown. The lady in the brown hat still eyes Jack with disdain.

Jack watches the numbers light up above the doors: They pass ten, and then twelve, then fourteen, and the car stops. The ladies get off. Then the mother and son pick up their bags, and they get off on fifteen. Jack follows them out. The boy takes a look at Jack and does a quick double take, probably recognizing him from *Shake 'Em Down*, but when he turns to say something to his mom, Jack cuts the other way down the carpeted hall, taking off for the vending machines and—he hopes—the stairway.

After a series of turns, Jack finds the entrance to the stairs. He checks the door to make sure it won't lock him in as soon as it's closed, and then heads up to the sixteenth floor. He's quieter now, more careful as he moves through the halls. He stops before rounding the corner to his room and takes a quick, stealthy look. As he'd hoped, no one's waiting for him in front of his door; it's a good thing he didn't use his real name.

Jack makes the turn and runs the last twenty feet to his room, fumbles with the card key to open the door, and then pushes it closed once he's inside. Only when he's done this does it occur to him that someone could have broken in and be waiting inside. But a fast look around shows him that's not the case.

Jack crosses to the desk by the window and opens the drawer

where he left the small revolver Freeman had given him after taking it off the suit in the alley. He never wanted to come to the point where he'd need it, but you're better off having a gun and not needing it than needing it and not having it. At least that's how Jack sees it.

He pops the cylinder to make sure the gun is still loaded: It is, but with two bullets spent. Jack slides it closed to an empty shell, so that when he cocks the hammer, a live round will rotate into the breech.

At a knock on the door, Jack wheels and listens. He hears Freeman's voice. "Housekeeping, Jack. Open the fucking door."

Jack looks around but doesn't move from where he is. Instead he thumbs back the gun's hammer.

"I saw you come up, Jack. Open the door, my man."

Jack swears under his breath. "Hey," he says, trying to sound casual. He starts over to the door and stops at the peephole. On the other side, he sees only Freeman, though that doesn't mean he's alone. The guy's big enough to cover a whole window; he easily fills the small amount of hallway Jack can see through the door's little peephole.

"You sneaking around on me, Jack?"

"I should be asking *you* that, big man."

Freeman's fist hits the door close to Jack's face, and Jack jumps back, raises the gun.

"How'd you know what room I was in?" The only way Freeman could know is if he followed Jack up last night after dropping him off.

"I—," Freeman says. "Didn't you tell me?"

"Yeah," Jack says. "But I don't think I did."

"Open the fucking door."

"You want to leave me ass-out in this mess, Free? Drop me by the side to save your own shit?"

"Open this fucking door, Jack."

"What're we doing today, Free? Going to see Alexi Akakievich at Prescott Court?"

"Make this easy, Jack. Face facts: You not going to be solving any big cases here. You not saving the city, your ass, any of that shit."

Jack puts his hand against the door, feels the grain of the wood between him and a man big enough to rip him apart.

"Mills is dead, Free. Your boys, whoever they are, they just blew him in half like they did O'Malley. The fifty caliber cannon, that's how they did him."

"Some shit, ain't it?"

Jack feels something hit the other side of the door. He looks through the peephole and sees Freeman pushing against it with his arm. "There going to be two sides in this thing, Jack: the big swinging dicks and the streets. Alexi Akakievich owns the streets. Which side you going to be on, your own? I'm not taking that side anymore. I only gamble when I know I'm gonna win."

Jack steps away from the door. He looks around the room. To one side is the bathroom, no exits there. On the other side of the room is a doorway that opens into the room next door. Jack pads across the carpet as quietly as he can, unlocks the latch, and opens the door. Behind it he finds another door, locked.

"You don't have a side in this now, Jack. Fact is, your ass gone get squeezed in the middle. I can't let that happen to me. This my *life* here."

Jack pushes against the locked door. If he could break it down and escape through the next room when Freeman breaks into his, he could possibly make it to the hall. But out in the hotel, with Freeman coming after him and the two Suits waiting somewhere, he probably wouldn't get to his car.

"You know I can break this door out, Jack. Why don't you come open it up now, make things easier?"

Jack faces the room's main door. He has his cell phone and Alvin Shaw's card in his pocket, but neither of them is going to do him any immediate good. Hotel security would never arrive in time. "So what am I supposed to do, Free? What's Akakievich going to do when you bring me in?"

"To who?" Freeman's laugh echoes out in the hall. "To you or to me?"

"Yeah. So what do I do?"

"Just open the door, man. Make this easier on us both."

Jack raises the gun and holds it with both hands, pointing it at the door. "I've got the gun, Free. Don't make me use it on you."

"You serious, Jack? Don't talk crazy." Out in the hall, Freeman pushes against the door. The frame creaks, but the door holds.

"I'm serious, Free."

"Don't kid yourself, Jack. This ain't no movie."

"If this was a movie, my friend wouldn't be selling me out."

"Open the door and we'll talk. You starting to piss me off."

Jack moves away from the door. He raises the gun and waits.

"Come on in, big man. Nothing to do now but take the next step."

With an insane yell, Freeman smashes into the door and the whole thing rattles. Jack sees the frame move in the wall. Freeman grunts and hits the door a second time, tearing the lock and the chain out of the frame. The door bangs open, slaps against a mirrored closet door, smashing the glass, and then falls closed again until Freeman stops it with his hand.

He steps into the room, his big face a mask of anger, one hand against the door and the other raised, his fingers spread and clenched like he's ready to pull Jack's limbs off his body.

But Jack's got him lined up, both hands on the gun and his arms level, the barrel pointed right at Freeman's chest.

22

Jack speaks with all the calm he can manage. "Close the door."

Freeman lets the door fall closed against what's left of the frame. It won't quite fit into place or lock again, but Jack relaxes a little when no one else comes in.

"Where are the Suits?"

Freeman lowers his arms as he stares at the barrel of the gun.

"Now, Jack, what you really going to do? Just come take a ride real quick. This all can end."

"With you and your friends? What'd you do with the Suits?"

"It's just us, Jack. That's how you want it, right? It's how I do."

Jack takes another step away from the big man. He judges Freeman's reach, steps toward the foot of the bed.

"What did you do last night after you dropped me off?"

"Just business, Jack." Freeman shakes his head, tilts his neck to one side until it pops. "We all have to do what we can do. Now, don't you see this little police charade ain't going to pan out? You not going to fix this, Jack."

"Who shot Mills?"

"Ain't that a bitch, though?" Freeman steps into the room as though this is only a casual chat, shaking his head and smiling at the news of another death.

Jack steps around the end of the bed, wanting to put the queen-size between them.

"Put down the gun, Jack. Don't be crazy about none of this." Freeman reaches toward Jack, steps closer again.

Jack feels his way along the end of the bed with his foot, keeping the gun and both eyes on Freeman. At the corner, he moves to the other side of the bed.

"Give me the gun, Jack."

Jack shakes the gun, aims it toward Freeman's knee. "You remember back at the Coast? How it felt to get shot in the leg?"

"Yeah. I remember. And I'm still standing." Freeman pushes out his lips. "You want to shoot me?" He holds his arms out wide from his waist. "Go ahead."

Maybe Jack waits a second too long; maybe Freeman gets tired of waiting. He steps up onto the bed to come at Jack, and Jack steps back. As he does, he pulls the trigger.

The gun goes off, loud and hot, blasting a slug through Freeman's left knee. Blood splatters onto the bedspread, and Freeman topples over the foot of the bed onto his back on the floor.

He reaches up as soon as he's down, clawing at the bed, pulling spread and blankets toward him as he tries to get up. Something awful, a growl in a register Jack's never heard a person use, bellows out through Freeman's teeth.

Jack shot a gun in his movie, went through a complete handgun training course in preparation for his role as Sergeant Mike Haggerty. But the truth is, he's never shot a person, and it was something he hoped he'd never have to do. Now he's crossed that line: There's a before and an after, and he's just come into the now.

"Yo, Jack," Freeman says, his whole face clenching in pain, "now I'm a have to kill you myself!"

"Violence," Jack says. "It only leads to more of the same."

Freeman shouts his pain, a sound Jack fears will be heard down the hall, will bring people running.

He steps up onto the bed, but as he does, Freeman yanks the blankets and sheets out from under him. Jack slides down and feels one of Freeman's strong hands clamp around his foot. Now he's being pulled toward the big man, and Jack crunches, reaches down toward Freeman's hand with his gun. He fires again, this time shooting from point blank range into the back of Freeman's forearm, maybe six inches above his wrist.

The big man screams again, falls back onto the floor.

"Fuck!"

Jack slides off the other side of the bed, stands between Freeman and the door.

"Let's call this done now. I walk out that door; this ends between us."

"Fuck! You think those fucking Russians aren't looking for you all over this hotel? They're coming to get your ass!"

"What did O'Malley do to fuck up?"

Freeman rolls over to sitting, still holding his arm. "He couldn't deliver. People be fucking with Akakievich, and he don't feel protected. He coming after the fucks who supposed to supply that protection. You hear?" Freeman gets one foot under him, the bad knee still making him wince in pain. It's his left side: both the knee and the arm. So Jack points the gun at his other side.

"You think you got any shot at the Hall of Fame?"

Freeman looks stunned. "*What?*"

"You got anything to keep that other knee for, pal? Because I wouldn't want to have to think I destroyed two Hall of Fame knees today."

"Fuck this." Freeman makes a move toward Jack, a straight on rush with his good hand out and the power coming from his good leg while the other leg trails the bedspread.

Before he can even think about it, Jack jumps back toward the door and opens it hard, hitting Freeman and knocking his arm out of the way. Jack steps out into the hallway and looks around: He sees no one.

He yanks against the door, losing what little composure he still has, and feels it knock into Freeman once more.

Jack doesn't want to feel the way he does, but his eyes are starting to go blurry and a part of him is raging inside, his blood pumping so loud he can hear it. "This ends between us."

Freeman's eyes are cold and hard, black between his lids, dead set on Jack and as serious as those of an animal trapped in its den.

"You hear me?"

When Freeman doesn't say anything, Jack steps back into the hall. With shots fired, it's only a matter of time until someone comes looking, whether it's the Russians or hotel security.

Jack takes a last look at Freeman and shakes his head. "I didn't want to do this, man," he says. "Seriously."

23

Jack pulls the door closed behind him. It hits against the frame but stays partly closed. If the Russians find Freeman, it's his own problem.

If they find Jack, he's fucked.

At the stairs, he opens the door with care and listens for steps echoing above or below in the stairwell. He hears nothing. Somewhere in the hotel, the two Russians have to be looking for him.

He starts down the stairs.

After a few flights, Jack realizes he's still holding the gun. He tucks it into the back of his pants.

On the eighth floor, he leaves the stairs and calls for an elevator. He gets a full look at himself in the doors' reflection: only a slight smear of blood on the side of his mouth. His shirt looks like he scraped it across a sidewalk downtown. It's his eyes that look the craziest, that hold something he's not at all used to and doesn't like.

The bell chimes, and Jack holds his breath, slips to the side of the doors with his hand behind his back, on the grip of the gun. The doors slide open to reveal a somewhat older woman, wearing a gray fur coat over a low-cut sweater. The cleavage she's sporting is of the decidedly saggy variety. Cradled in her left arm is a small dog in a wicker bag.

Jack steps in and farts. He'd felt it coming but does nothing to make it quiet.

The woman snorts, trains her eyes on the front of the car.

The small dog barks at Jack.

"Oh," he says, "I didn't realize they let animals stay at the hotel." Perhaps this is how Sergeant Haggerty would act.

At the lobby, Jack hides against the wall of the car, giving the woman his biggest smile as she gets off fast. He hits the button for G2, the level where he parked the Fastback. If the Russians are smart, that's where at least one of them will be waiting. But the garage has three levels, and Jack's counting on them not knowing which one he'll be on.

The elevator doors open at G2, and Jack steps out into the bright fluorescent-white garage. He listens for a moment but doesn't hear anything. Now he's starting to worry that the Russians have something else going on or they're smarter than he's given them credit for.

This isn't the time to be second-guessing his luck.

The Fastback's still where he left it, in the middle of a row, the parking voucher still on the seat. Out of habit, Jack touches the hole in the door as he opens the lock. He still hates the fact that the Fastback got shot, but there's something soothing about the way the tip of his finger fits into the bare metal hole. He's come to accept the imperfections in the car's shell, like he has the blemishes in his life.

That, or he's nostalgic for the days when people shot at him with normal-size guns, when a bullet hole wasn't a crater big enough to put your whole hand through.

Then Jack's knees feel weak and he holds the car with both hands, leans against it. A hot rush of blood passes through his head, and he sees the image of Freeman's knee exploding in a bloody mess. He sees Freeman's eyes again, the way they filled with hate and then resignation. He shakes his head, hard, trying to clear it.

The air in the garage suddenly feels stale, empty. As soon as he gets the door open, Jack collapses into the big leather seat, feels the weight of his body slipping away.

He takes a few deep breaths, looks down at the black steering wheel and the small indentations around it, then starts the machine. He hears the sound and feels the vibration of the car's big engine. He gives it gas and listens to the 289 cubic inch V8 purr and then growl. The sound fills the garage, its vibrations setting off a couple of alarms.

"That's good," Jack says. The roar of the Mustang: It's what he needs to hear.

He makes his way up the two levels to the street entrance, watching all around him, ready to gun the engine if he sees any Russians in gray suits. But he doesn't. At the booth, he feeds in his ticket and the gate rises in front of him, leaving an unobstructed path to the street.

Before he makes his way into traffic, he takes a long look down the sidewalk, scanning the entrances in front of the hotel. Sure enough, the two Russian Suits are standing in front of the main door, both looking pissed. Jack rolls down his window. He knows it's not cool, not the best move for a smart, streetwise investigator, but he really can't resist.

"Hey, guys," Jack calls out. He honks the big American 1960s horn—a foghorn compared to the sounds that come out of today's cars. It takes them a second, Mr. Gray Suit and Mr. Gray Suit, but then they look his way, and he gives them the finger. "Go fuck yourselves," he says, making a right turn onto the street.

He can see them give chase for maybe ten feet, and then he gets into third gear, heading for Market during a relative lull in traffic, and they disappear behind him in the crowds.

24

Jack calls the number on the back of Alvin Shaw's card as soon as he gets over the Bay Bridge. It goes to voicemail, and he leaves a message, saying he's a friend of Mills Hopkins. Jack has no idea where else to go, so he keeps on toward Walnut Creek.

When he's passing through Oakland on 24, he gets a call from Shaw's cell.

"Thanks for calling back."

"What's this about?" the cop asks.

Ahead of him, Jack can see green hills with a ridge of fog trapped up against them. This is where the mist comes in off the Bay and then builds up as clouds or fog—take your pick. The clouds will dump the heavy moisture and then move east over the hills into the dry, sunny country beyond.

"Mills Hopkins said I should make contact."

On the other end of the phone, Shaw grunts. Jack keeps on. "Something bad happened to him this morning. I'm not sure if we'll be seeing him again."

"You know anything about that, I need you to come in."

"I was there."

"What I said, then. How soon can you meet me at the station in Walnut Creek?"

Jack's about to answer when the cop cuts him off. "You can trust me," he says.

In Walnut Creek, Jack finds the station and parks outside. He studies the small building: brick with a peaked roof and trimmed bushes out front, a hundred times friendlier than San Francisco's Hall of Justice. Here brick steps lead up to the building, and there are no statues of Justice with her scales carved into the wall. It gives you less reverence for the law maybe, but if that comes with less fear then that's fine with Jack.

As far as he knows, he hasn't been followed. He checked his rearview mirror enough times to see about every car that was behind him from the hotel to Walnut Creek, and none of them were recurring offenders. Maybe it's not a pro job of checking for a tail, but it's the best Jack can do.

Jack gets out of the Fastback and shakes a cigarette out of his pack. He's early, still has ten minutes before he's supposed to meet with the cop. He lights up, watching cops and other people walk in and out of the station. Everything seems busy for a Saturday. After a few drags, Jack figures his safety's not worth the small indulgence. He snuffs out the cigarette and heads inside.

"Yo, easy rider," calls a black cop with a shaved head when Jack gets up to the homicide division. He'd recognize the gruff voice from the phone even if this guy didn't have a sign on his desk that says he's Shaw. The cop stands up, and Jack can see he's built like his voice: his tan polo shirt stretched tight across his pecs and shoulders, the short sleeves even tighter around his arms. The leather straps of a shoulder holster are visible around both shoulders. This guy's all cop—younger than Hopkins, but the same breed upgraded. Even his mustache is tight, and his bald pate gleams.

"Shaw," Jack says, coming forward and extending his hand.

"The movie star. So what's up with your hair?"

"Sorry. It's bad." Jack touches the too-long locks behind his head, aware he's sporting a nasty salad. "But I haven't had a chance to cut it. I was on the road and—"

"Come on." Shaw hits Jack's arm with a bunch of papers and is already on the move, walking toward the stairs. "Lucky for you we have a barber down the basement of the station. One of the benefits of the 'burbs. Seriously, your shit looks like shit, Jack. When we get you down there, we can talk."

Sure enough, in the basement of the station is a small barbershop: three big old-fashioned leather chairs and one old barber with a white smock and a hot lather machine on the shelf by his mirror. They get Jack set up in the middle chair, the sheet around his neck, and Shaw sits down in the next chair.

"Short?" the barber asks, his voice a little strange.

"Ahh, yeah."

The man takes out his clippers to go to work.

"So tell me what happened to our friend."

"Anyone make a report?"

"They just faxed over forensics from Vaillancourt Fountain ten minutes ago. Hell of a big hole there and a shit ton of blood. Witness said he saw some guy from a movie. But he couldn't remember the dude's name." Shaw smiles. "And no mention of Mills in the report."

"Because he was gone by the time anyone showed. Someone put him in a trunk and drove off."

Shaw watches Jack's eyes in the mirror, meets his gaze with an intense stare. "Someone shot the shit out of that place. Witnesses in the report don't mention you as a target, but they identified a"—Shaw makes air quotes as he says the words—"B-list movie star." He smiles. "So pretty soon someone puts your name to that and you got people wanting to ask you questions."

"How would I—"

"Relax, Jack. That's why it's good you came here. Hopkins told me about you; I know you couldn't have been down on the scene shooting a Barrett M107. So don't worry about the SF cops right now. They're a whole other world away."

"But?" Jack looks around at the barbershop. Above them is a whole station of police officers.

Shaw shakes his head. "Technically, you're not even in the station right now."

The barber touches the base of Jack's neck with the clippers, and Jack jumps.

Shaw picks at a stack of magazines. The barber pats Jack's shoulder, his eyes calm in the mirror, and brings the clippers up to Jack's neck again. Their vibration sends a chill down Jack's spine.

"Let him cut your hair. This is a good time for you to start looking a little different—not that anyone won't recognize you after a second anyway." Shaw pauses his search through the magazines to look up. "So tell me what it was like to star in a big Hollywood movie."

"What?"

"Technically, we're not even talking. We're just two guys sitting next to each other in a barber shop." He lifts a magazine and starts to flip through the pages.

Jack looks in the mirror at the barber and then at Shaw. He waits for Shaw to lower his magazine—*Guns and Ammo*—and then makes eye contact.

"Who, him?" Shaw asks. "You can say anything in front of Lou that you'd say in the privacy of your own home. Isn't that right, Lou?"

Jack watches the barber stay focused on his hair, buzzing away the dirty locks of the road.

"He's deaf," Shaw says. "Reads lips like a wonder, but if he's not watching you? Forget it. You might as well be talking in Dutch."

Jack laughs his quick laugh, a puff of air coming out his nose—all nerves.

"Tell me where the shots were coming from."

"I can't be sure. I heard a car speed away when it was over, but I don't know if you could—"

"You couldn't shoot a gun that size out of a car unless you had a steel mount built into the door. And I don't know anyone who'd want that much profile on their vehicle. Do you?"

"No, I—"

"SF is checking the surrounding area for casings, but they won't find any. They'll find lots of potential places a shooter could've sighted from, but no casings. Not this guy."

"You know the guy from his gun?"

"Give this boy a prize. You know who's got the Barrett M107? Serious motherfuckers who don't screw around and the FBI. You want to take a shot at which one it could've been?"

"What?"

"Exactly." Shaw puts down the magazine and looks at Jack in the mirror. "Now listen. In a minute someone you don't know is going to come in here and sit in that other chair." He points to the empty chair on Jack's left. "That person is your friend. Whatever you may think, do not doubt that."

"Who is?" Jack shuffles to get up, but Shaw puts his hand on Jack's forearm.

"Relax. You're not going anywhere, and you don't need to go yet. Get your fucking haircut. If you leave now, you'll look like a freak." He points to the mirror at Jack's hair, half shaved, half long and greasy. "You're looking better already."

Jack's starting to look like his old self: His forehead's appearing with a pronounced tan line across it, but he's looking younger without all the curls.

"Thing is," says a soft voice behind Jack, "all of San Francisco's pissed off right now."

A woman walks from the entrance of the shop toward the chair on Jack's left. She's got long blond hair, sports nice, understated makeup and wears a navy blue business suit with a white shirt underneath. Her collar's splayed out to show a glimpse of gold—a necklace as well as the skin beneath it. It's the Fed from the scene of the second dead girl.

"The whole PD. Truly. More so than with O'Malley. Let's just say O'Malley had his enemies. Now, Sergeant Hopkins on the other hand,"—she sits down in the empty chair, looks Jack dead-on in the mirror—"he had people on his side. And now they all want you for his murder."

25

For a second, Jack has a Mohawk. Then the barber takes a last run over Jack's scalp, back to front, and the last of his long hair falls from the middle of his head.

"This is Federal Agent Jane Gannon," Shaw says. "She and I are the only ones who know you're here."

"Call me Jane." She touches Jack's wrist, all smiles.

Jack feels like he's walked into the bad guy's lair, almost like they've strapped him down and are telling him their sinister plan.

"How do you two know each other?"

They look at each other and smile. Shaw says, "Oh, we go way back. Met down in Central America about that thing."

She nods. "Right. *That* thing."

"It's okay," Shaw says. "We're all friends of Mills's."

"Are we?" Jack looks at the two of them. "Then tell me what the hell's going on."

Gannon shakes her head. "Tsk-tsk, Jack. No need to get so upset. What we're doing?" She fixes Jack with her baby blues in the mirror. "Is we're protecting your ass. Because if we didn't—"

She holds up her hand to cut off his interruption.

"Because if we didn't, you'd be nine-tenths of the way to

getting yourself killed or thrown in jail. Ultimately you'd probably get both."

"How do I know I can trust—"

"That's not the right question for this moment, Jack. What you should be asking is how we're going to keep you safe."

Shaw adds, "That or who you're about to get killed by."

Jack turns to Shaw, but the barber catches his head and straightens it out. He's bringing the tight trimmer along the back of Jack's neck. "Akakievich, probably," he says. "Him and some corrupt insider cops with a fifty caliber sniper rifle. Is that right?"

"But what we don't know," Gannon says, "is who the corruption starts with and how far it runs."

"How do you plan to find out?"

Shaw starts shaking his head.

"Well," she says. "We could follow you around and see who sends you to the morgue, but we think there might be a better way."

Jack feels the buzzer tickle his skin below the hair line and hopes the cut will be over soon. "Try me."

"Well," she says. "*I* think we should work together."

Jack knows that he's in no position to negotiate, that these two are probably his only chance on the street. Still, he can't go along unless he knows who or what he's working with.

"So you're FBI," Jack says. "Why are the Feds involved here? What's your angle?"

Gannon winces. "I'm afraid—"

Shaw cuts in. "It's okay, Jane."

She shakes her head. "I'm afraid that's not open for discussion."

"Then what?" Jack asks. "Tell me why you were there when O'Malley got shot."

Shaw catches Gannon's eye in the mirror, and even with the barber lining up his sideburns—long still, but straight across—Jack sees the look they exchange plain as day. Something goes between them in that instant. Then Gannon looks at her hand, eyes a ring on her finger that would make a diamond buyer jealous.

"You're right," she says. "I was there. But now I'm the one who doesn't trust this location."

***

When the cut's finished, the barber won't let Jack pay for his haircut. "It's covered by the department," Shaw explains. But that doesn't stop Jack from tucking a twenty-dollar tip into the guy's coat pocket.

"Anything you can do about this jacket?" Jack says, eyeing himself in the mirror on their way out of the shop. The leather's seen much better days.

Shaw shakes his head and laughs. "Don't think so, pal. Looks like you'll be our biker dude for a little while yet."

"But don't worry," Gannon says. "That look is in style."

Jack laughs uneasily, always ready to go along with a joke at his own expense.

Shaw leads them through a side door off the barber shop, around to the back of the station where a black Town Car with tinted windows is parked. Gannon unlocks it with a remote and walks around to the driver's side. Jack and Shaw get in, Shaw taking the front.

Jack asks where they're going as Gannon starts the engine.

"It's okay" is all Shaw says.

Gannon starts to drive, making her way along the streets of Walnut Creek, away from the station and the Fastback. Jack watches his car through the rear window as it recedes from view.

"Is my—"

"It's *all* okay, Jack."

They drive streets Jack doesn't recognize. All he knows about Walnut Creek is the mall, and he's seen some residential streets the few times he's gotten lost looking for the highway.

"So at the mall," Gannon begins, watching the road but checking Jack's eyes in the rearview mirror. "O'Malley was ready to come in. We'd been talking to him for a while, and then in the middle of the night, he calls me and says he's ready to come in. Wants to spill his info and go into protection. Nobody was *supposed* to know. But somebody did."

"O'Malley was shooting at my house a few hours before that," says Jack. "He fucks up and then has a big moralistic change of heart? Nice fucking guy."

"That's how it is sometimes." She looks back in the mirror and meets Jack's eyes. "Sometimes we're an all-night operation. Guy figures he's gone too far, he's in too deep with something, we get the call. Whenever. *Wherever.*"

"But then he gets dead."

"We make the meet at his car. I see the girl in the back and know something's gone wrong. Very wrong. He was coked to the gills, jumpy. Waving a gun around because he thought someone was going to get him.

"Then someone takes his head off with a cannon. I was lucky

it didn't hit me too. Lucky O'Malley didn't shoot me. His gun went off and blew out the windshield. I look out and try to find someone to shoot at, but there's not a damn thing there. Just black night."

"Then you walk away," Jack says. "Leave the body for the police to find."

She nods. "If we had taken over the case at that point, it would have let too many people know the FBI was involved. We didn't want to tip our hand. We still don't."

"But you walked away instead of running like you might get shot at. I interviewed witnesses who say you walked away calm as ice."

Shaw tips his head toward Jack. "Boy does some homework. You have to give him that."

Gannon shrugs. "You see a bullet like that tear a man's head off, you know a sniper's got you. There's not much you can do but walk away. If he wants you, you're his."

Jack thinks back to the scene that morning at Vaillancourt Fountain. Maybe running saved his life, or maybe—he realizes—the sniper didn't want him dead.

He takes a closer look at Gannon: beautiful, not a woman he'll be forgetting anytime soon. But a woman he can believe? She looks good—maybe better than someone in the FBI should. The government wouldn't waste a looker like her on a porn-ring investigation any more than a San Francisco cop should be driving a fully loaded Saleen Mustang. She should be schmoozing international playboys and spies. Jack still has doubts—doubts he'll keep to himself.

It's starting to get dark outside. Lights are coming on in front of the houses. Another Saturday night in the suburbs. "Okay. Start at the beginning. Explain this to me like I'm a six-year-old child."

26

Jane Gannon shrugs. She angles the Town Car over to the side of the road and pulls to a stop outside a gated community, one full of identical condos with brown shingles. She parks and turns around in her seat to eye Jack.

"We knew that O'Malley was in deep with Akakievich and that he wasn't the only one involved from the force. He came to us and said that he'd been inside, undercover, then Akakievich asked him to go after cops and his connection from above suggested he do it. That he was afraid for his life if he didn't."

"You know that's all bullshit, right?"

Jane tilts her head from side to side. "Sometimes you have to listen," she says. "You buy into what they tell you, and then they come in and you get the real story, you work them for more."

"Okay. So what did he give you that *wasn't* bullshit?"

"He said that Akakievich wasn't happy anymore, that out of the blue, he'd gotten pissed about the whole operation. He wanted more—types of protection O'Malley couldn't deliver. O'Malley wasn't sure what Akakievich would do next."

"So he tried to off me to clean up his balance?"

"O'Malley had been sent a message that he wasn't needed anymore. He knew he was expendable, but he figured he could earn some points by removing a problem: you."

In the front seat, Shaw coughs. He turns around to look at Jack. "O'Malley's watching something that gets too big for him. He's got people above him on the force who he can't trust. He knows they're getting squeezed and isn't sure where he stands. So he decides to go outside. He goes federal."

Jack waits to hear if Gannon will support this idea. When nothing comes, he says, "O'Malley felt the squeeze starting to come down, and he wanted out. But he wasn't running from anything he didn't get himself into."

Gannon says, "We got involved here because we know he's not the only one. Something starts to look bad enough, it's bigger than the city level, even IA, then that's when we get brought in. Calls get made. We were onto that even before we made contact with O'Malley."

"And that's when Mills comes in. He gets my tip on O'Malley, and Akakievich gets rattled by the cops. Akakievich gets upset and wants more from his partners inside."

"Exactly." Gannon nods at Shaw like Jack might actually be showing them something. "Hopkins had been watching O'Malley, trying to get Internal Affairs to close him out. But it wasn't working. IA couldn't get anything to stick. Who knows what the fuck goes on with those guys. O'Malley's connection up above, the guy *really* calling the shots, he didn't want this thing going down, so he shut him up. *He* is the one we need to find."

Shaw nods. "That's it. Who sent this case to Walnut Creek, who kept IA off O'Malley, and who wanted Hopkins dead. It's Akakievich running things, but he's getting help from the inside."

"Hopkins stepped in the way of that big swinging dick, then got hit with the shaft."

"Nice image," Shaw says. "You next?"

"But this gets worse, Jack."

"What am I missing?"

Gannon turns all the way around in her seat to meet his eyes directly. "In a day or less, Hopkins's death is going to come up solved by the SFPD."

"I see where this is going." Jack knows he's not going to like what she says next.

"They'll be closing the case with you as the killer. The only questions then will be whether they can find you, and if they do, whether they take you into custody alive."

27

Shaw smiles a row of white beneath his mustache. "This is where you thank us for protecting you."

"We'll bring you to a safe house," Gannon says, "until we can find O'Malley's man higher up."

"Freeman said that it went all the way to the top, that there was more than one city official tied in with Akakievich's house rules."

"Who's this?"

"Freeman Jones. Guy was working with me but now he's not. Matter of fact, I just shot him."

Gannon smiles. "Nice."

She makes a few phone calls, and it becomes clear that no one turned up at the scene of Jack's hotel room. Somehow, shot up and with that much noise in the hotel, the big man managed to get away. But it doesn't take long for Gannon to track down a tattoo-faced Samoan with NFL Players Association insurance and a couple of bullets in him. He's at the Kaiser on Geary.

"Tell them to keep him there," she tells the agent on the other end of the phone. She's already moving the car, turning it around.

"I don't think he'll be going anywhere fast," Jack says.

At the hospital, Gannon's man has already had Freeman moved to a private room and his drugs cut off. A fresh-faced Fed is standing outside in the hall when they arrive. Freeman's awake and aware. All they have to do is close the door to get him alone.

"Hello, Mr. Jones," Shaw says as soon as they walk in. "Or should I call you *Freakman*?"

The room is the standard white hospital box with windows on one side. Jack sees half a city of buildings and then a hill lined with little white houses. The big man looks whiter in the face and thinner somehow, like they hung him upside down and bled him dry. It's probably not so far from the truth.

Jack sees his own reflection in the room's big dark window. *He* did this. He's the one who caused it all.

Freeman's big head turns on the pillow to face the threesome. His mouth thins, breaks into a wry smile. "Fuck you, Jack."

Jack backs away from the bed. "I'm sorry, Free."

"Listen, Mr. Jones." Gannon flips out a wallet and waves her ID in front of Freeman's face. "I'm Jane Gannon with the Federal Bureau of Investigation. And Mr. Palms has already told us about seeing you go into Akakievich's establishment on Prescott Court. So, please, let's be straightforward with each other."

Freeman's voice is strained as he says, "Or what?" He holds up his good hand and the white-bandaged forearm of his left arm. "What can you do to me now?"

"Well," she says, "I count five fingers there that I could ask Officer Shaw here to break for you."

Freeman laughs out loud. "I freaking love you guys. Jack, you believe these two? This blond killed the cop in Walnut Creek, right?"

Jack steps forward. "Guys," he says. "Is that really necessary?"

"I'm the bad guy for talking to Akakievich, but you hanging with corrupt cops isn't worse? A killer Fed?"

Shaw steps forward and takes off his jacket, revealing his tight shirt and the muscles around his neck and shoulders. "Talk to us, big man. We want to know who Akakievich is working with on the inside. What do you know about his connects to the San Francisco police?"

Gannon rests her hand on Freeman's shoulder. "And let me add, Mr. Jones, that it'll be pretty clear to anyone who's watching that we were here. Who knows? Maybe we leave and they think you didn't tell us anything. Then again, maybe they think you did." She smiles as sweet as you'd imagine. Gives a small feminine shrug.

"Yeah, fuck it," Freeman says. "Any port, right? Will you guys protect my ass and give me immunity on this all?"

Gannon nods. "I will do everything in my power. You can be assured of that. But we need to know what you know."

Jack starts to say something about not trusting the big man, but he stops himself. Better to stay out of the way now.

Freeman chuckles. Already he's getting some of his color back, as if talking is bringing him back to life. Jack steps toward the wall, hoping to stay out of sight. "Fuck. I seen a cop in the house. Asian guy."

"He's SFPD? You know his name?" Shaw asks.

Freeman shakes his head. "Never heard anyone call his name. But I seen him hanging around North Beach with O'Malley. Those two just cruise it together. Find who his partner was. That be your start."

Gannon nods. "What's he look like?"

"A relatively big dude. Wide. Has an Asian mullet, you know what I mean? He's one of the boys, but you know, he thinks he's big."

"Matsumoto," Gannon says.

Freeman nods. "Maybe. Yeah." Then he laughs. "The shit is, you fucks probably the only ones in the city who don't know what's up here. That, or maybe you the only ones still ain't getting paid off." Freeman smiles at Gannon. "Not that I know if I should believe that about you, Fed Lady. Then again, guess I don't have much choice about whether I should believe you." He winks. "Got to play along, right?"

Shaw's back muscles tense as he makes fists with both hands. "Cut this bullshit and speak your mind."

Freeman stops as if he's considering whether to stop talking altogether. Then he says, "Shit be all around North Beach, man. Word gets around about what Akakievich is running and not to fuck with it. He trying to put the squeeze on Franklin Clarence. You want to know how high this goes? How about all the way up."

"Shit," Shaw says.

Even Jack knows that Franklin Clarence is the chief of the San Francisco police.

"Clarence been getting his joint waxed at the Top Notch for more than a year now. That's how come Akakievich can do whatever the fuck he wants. O'Malley? He Clarence's bitch."

"Will you testify—"

"Oh, *hell* no. You won't never see me again you try some shit like that. You want somebody to fix this, you going to have to catch these motherfuckers red-handed."

Gannon looks sideways back at Jack. She squints as though

she's not sure why he's backed away.

"And that'll never happen," she says. "Because Akakievich is starting to clean out that inventory as we speak. Is that right?"

Freeman pushes his lips out, then says, "Don't ask me." He holds up his arm. "Fuck with my bullet holes if you want to, I don't know shit about that."

Shaw catches Freeman by the elbow and the hand, cradles his arm as if inspecting the bandages. "Be careful what you wish for."

Freeman yanks his arm away. "Akakievich *pissed*," he says. "First this motherfucker"—he points at Jack with his chin—"and don't think I forgotten you over there."

Jack wishes Freeman weren't talking to him, but there's not much choice but to meet the big man's stare head on. "I'm here."

"Yeah. This motherfucker fuck shit up at the Coast, and then Mills Hopkins be snooping around." Now Freeman raises his good hand. "But don't think he don't know about you all too." He points at Gannon. "Soon as the Feds came in, that's when he got pissed with the situation. That's why he pissed at Clarence. Plus he trying to get new ground at Mission Bay. Wants to start a whole new red-light district over there."

"How—"

"Don't fool yourself. He just know. You Feds come in, that's when Akakievich start cleaning out girls. Right now, he getting ready to move his location. Making Clarence grease some paperwork. That's what I saw when I went in there; Prescott Court fit to shut the doors."

Shaw folds his arms. He looks toward Jack, then back to Freeman. "Are you saying—"

"Yeah. This whole shit about to come down."

28

They sit in Gannon's car again, the heat on and Jack in the front seat this time.

Gannon has her BlackBerry out, typing into it or scrolling through e-mails, Jack's not quite sure. She's either trying to decide whom to contact or she already has and is telling them what she knows.

Finally Gannon looks up from the screen and turns to Shaw. "I want to know how Akakievich found out about the Bureau's involvement. Who could've clued him in on that?"

"That I don't know."

"I don't like the talk about this thing escalating," she says, "not for what it might do to the city or these girls. We have to make our move."

"I'm in," Jack says.

They both laugh, and Shaw pats Jack's shoulder from behind. "It's okay, man. No need for acting now."

"I—"

Gannon cuts him off. "This is what we do: Shaw goes to check out Prescott Court in North Beach, see if the big guy was right about Akakievich making his move. I'll do my best to get some manpower to make a raid. I want to get in fast and get out as many girls as we can."

"You don't want to go in together now?"

"If I could get thirty men I can trust? Sure. I'd take it. But there's no point in going after Prescott if Akakievich already knows we're coming."

Shaw nods as he zips up his leather jacket. "Ain't that a motherfuck of a feeling?" He shakes his head.

"I'll take Palms back to our safe house. Then we see what we can do about getting some help."

Shaw nods at Jack. "You call me if this guy gives you any trouble." He shoots Jack a last look and then gets out of the car.

Gannon takes a compact out of her purse and checks herself in the mirror, brings out a lipstick in a silver case and traces the lines of her lips. She looks good, and she knows it. Jack takes his time getting an eyeful.

"So, Jack Palms," she says, still checking her mirror. "You come out of hiding a couple of months back and help some Czech freewheelers secure a major coke buy." She tucks the compact into her purse and levels her glare at Jack. "Why is that?"

Jack starts to answer, and she holds up her hand. "Wait, I want to make sure I get the whole picture laid out here."

"Okay by me."

"Good. So you do your movie, drugs, tabloid routine and then disappear for close to three years. You come back and broker a drug buy that winds up in one of San Francisco's biggest bloodbaths in recent history. About half of the players involved get shot to bits, including Junius Ponds and Tony Vitelli. But you walk out clean as white sugar."

Jack bites his lips, both unsure and uncomfortable about where this is going.

"At one point, you even convince Sergeant Hopkins to spring Mr. Ponds to help you with this?" Her eyes go tight, like she really wants Jack to confirm this detail. Jack nods.

"And that doesn't raise any suspicions about anything that had or has gone on?"

Jack pushes himself deep into the leather seat. "Mills was...Mills took a risk for me."

"And how'd that pay off?" Jack can see the muscles in Gannon's neck move as she speaks.

"I thought at the time it went right. We left the scene with Akakievich in police custody, and I was able to turn over O'Malley's name. Plus Tony Vitelli was a son of a bitch who deserved to die."

Gannon leans closer. "And then you took a little motorcycle joy ride for more than a month with these drug buyers you brokered the deal for. Who, as far as I know, killed Mr. Vitelli themselves. Is that true?"

Jack feels like he's in the principal's office and he's about to get something way worse than detention.

"You're lucky," Gannon says, "that those Czechs have some of the right sort of friends."

"What?"

"These friends of yours, especially Vlade Kladivo and Niki Vojacek, talk to us." She raises her eyebrows. "Let's just say *they* are the primary reason we are here in San Francisco looking at Mr. Akakievich and his role in this city."

Now Jack sits forward, closer to Gannon. "*Really?*"

He wonders what the hell Vlade, Niki, and Al are doing talking to the Feds.

"Yes. And what you might find even more unbelievable: They have been telling us some very good things about you."

29

Gannon turns the radio to a jazz station as she pulls out of the hospital parking lot in the direction of downtown.

"So what becomes of me at this safe house?"

She tilts her head away from Jack, takes one hand off the wheel. "Well, that remains to be seen, I suppose."

Jack watches the road for a little while, thinks about his trust issues and his record with women. He lowers the window. "Mind if I smoke?"

She removes her own pack from a purse in the center console. "I thought you'd never ask."

With the windows down, they smoke in silence, working through their own thoughts as they make their way through San Francisco one red light at a time. After a while, Gannon asks, "So, was Hollywood life all that people make it out to be?"

"No," Jack says. "It was more."

She laughs, takes a long drag of her cigarette, and speaks before she's exhaled. "So what was it then?" she asks in a strained voice.

"It was too much: too many parties, too much excess, too much of the good, you know? It burned me out."

"No. Tell me about too much."

"The tabloids blew it all out of proportion. I got strung out, drugged out way too many days of the week, weeks to months, too much to do and too many places to go." He shrugs. "I lost track of it all. Then for three years I had to pay the price."

"You and your wife?"

"No." He shakes his head. "She's long gone." He looks at Gannon as she drives. She carefully angles the cigarette tip out into the wind, ashing it without tapping. "You telling me that you don't know this? That you didn't read about her charging me with assault?"

"Oh, I read it," she says. "Now I want to hear your version, give you a chance to clear your name."

"It is what it is. She drank too much, and I did whatever I could get my hands on. We fucked things up. But I never hit her, and now that part of my life is over." He goes back to looking out the window.

"Same with Ralph Anderino and the Czechs?" Jack waits to hear the rest, watches two blocks go by before she says, "You never did anything with them?"

"It was more like a job," he tells her. "Same as when I started on this O'Malley thing. Just me trying to play a role."

"Funny," she says, a serious look on her face. "I'd have thought you could find an easier way to make money."

"Yeah," Jack says, "I was thinking the same thing about you."

Jack sucks a long drag off his cigarette and flips the butt out the window. The sooner they get to the safe house, the better. He's had enough of women, especially when he's not sure where he stands.

This is work, he tells himself. Just go along, get through, and keep yourself alive. That's all you have to do.

***

When they're almost to the Bay, Gannon turns into an underground garage beneath one of the condo skyscrapers off the Embarcadero. They're probably only a few blocks from where Jack met Sergeant Hopkins so much earlier in the day.

One level down, she slides the car into a reserved spot and takes a Nextel phone out of her purse as she's shutting off the engine. The yellow phone beeps. "I'm here," she says into it. "Coming upstairs now with Palms."

The phone beeps again. "We're ready for you," a man's voice says.

Jack opens the car door and gets out. In the dim fluorescent light of the garage, he sees an exit on the far side.

"You thinking about trying to go out on your own?" she asks from the other side of the car. "Go ahead."

Jack turns to see she has him fixed in her stare. She runs a hand through her hair, exhales a hard long breath. "You still don't trust me?"

"Tell me one thing: If Akakievich knows the Feds are onto him and you might have a leak on your team, how do you know I'll be safe here at a Bureau location?"

She nods. "You wouldn't. That's why I brought you to my home."

30

Going up in the elevator to the fortieth floor, Jack keeps his eyes trained on the numbers above the door. If the doors were reflective, he'd check how he's holding up, but the whole elevator's made out of dark mahogany with gold trim. Class.

As soon as the doors open and Gannon steps out into the hall, Jack hears "Mommy!" A little girl runs up and jumps into Jane Gannon's outstretched arms. Gannon sweeps her up, spins her around, the two of them all smiles.

The simple pleasures, Jack thinks: home, love, kids.

He's surprised a federal agent has the confidence in her own safety to go ahead and have them. But life, he knows, doesn't wait for anyone.

Jack sees a tall man with dark hair standing in a doorway farther down the hall. He's clean-cut, wears a T-shirt advertising a local basketball league. As Gannon carries her daughter down the hall, the girl points at Jack. "Who's this?"

"This is our new friend, Jack."

Her husband offers Jack his hand. "Tom Gannon. Pleasure."

Inside the condo, Jack finds more dark wood and ceiling-to-floor windows looking out over downtown and the Bay. The scene is impressive.

"We're lucky," Tom says, as if he's read Jack's mind. "It's one of the perks. You know, with both of us working for the Bureau."

"Two agents?" Jack asks. "A family of Feds?"

Gannon turns, holding her daughter. "No more talking about that, okay?" She kisses her husband on the cheek. "Mr. Palms here doesn't need to know more about us."

"Fine," Tom says. He raises his eyebrows at Jack. "How about a drink?"

"Just water."

Tom winks at Jack and turns toward the kitchen. "Still on the wagon, huh? A smart man."

"I'm taking this one to bed." Jane carries their daughter down the hall.

"We never suspected someone as big as Clarence was involved in this mess." Tom opens a cabinet and takes out a glass.

Now Jack knows who Jane was e-mailing on her BlackBerry in the car. She calls to her husband from down the hall, asking him to come put their daughter to bed.

"Excuse me." Tom hands Jack a glass and points toward the sink. "Duty calls."

When Gannon comes back, she looks hard at Jack and asks if he doesn't want something stronger.

Jack holds up his glass. "I'm okay."

"So let me fill you in. That way we can make a move when we need to." She opens a cabinet and takes down a tall bottle of Talisker.

"Freeman told me it's the white girls. That's the big draw."

She gets a low glass out of the cabinet and fills it with ice. "More or less. The Eastern European connection satisfies the city's demand for white girls. But it's more complicated than that: You squeeze the Asian sex trade, you can imagine how they feel about it. So Alexi's operation is high cost, high risk.

"Still, the upside…" She waits until she has Jack's undivided attention. "Is that demand goes high enough that he can ask any price he wants. Not money, but power. And real estate."

"From the big swinging dicks."

She winces as she pours two fingers of scotch. "Nice." She takes a sip of the scotch, and it makes Jack want to have a smoke.

"You guys have a balcony or something here?"

"Come on."

She leads him down a darkened hallway toward the bedrooms, stopping to kiss her daughter goodnight. Even for two agents in the Bureau, the U.S. government doesn't pay this well. The Gannons have a crystal table, leather couches, fine mahogany built-in bookshelves, and a flat-screen TV mounted into the wall. It doesn't come out all clean, not the way Jack sees it. It makes him think of O'Malley driving the Saleen.

They make their way through the master bedroom, past a huge bed—solid wood headboard, a nice soft carpet, the whole room immaculately clean—and out onto a small corner balcony.

She slides the door closed when they're outside. The balcony can't be more than four feet by four feet: It's cozy and the two of them are close. The wind whips around the building—especially this high up, the wind is the coldest thing about the city. The wind and the fog. Tonight the fog is thick.

Jack pulls out his pack, offers her one, but she's already got a cigarette of her own between her lips. She lights it and offers Jack the cupped flame. But before he can mouth a cigarette out of his pack, the match goes out. She lights another one with Jack's help, his hands shielding it from the wind.

He takes a long drag. "Tell me about the girls. Tell me what this is all really about."

Gannon gulps back a good pull of scotch.

"It started small enough," she says. She stares out toward the Bay, her hair blowing around her face. "Just a few young girls coming over: dancing, pouring drinks, and Akakievich sets up his first club. Call it the Playboy Club meets *Barely Legal*. He starts expanding when word hits the streets he's got these underage white girls. Young virgins, no STDs, clean from Kiev. The first time is his best money. This town is fucked up, Jack, what can I say? The price starts going north. Pretty soon only the guys with the deepest pockets can afford to buy their way in. We're talking tens of thousands of dollars."

"What?"

"Yeah. This gets big. Guys are buying in as fast as Akakievich can bring the girls over. That's when things change." She takes a long drag and blows into the wind. "That's when it starts to be more about power."

"But we're still talking about a small club here. Right?"

Gannon shakes her head. "Akakievich still has a regular club, but he isn't content being a pimp. He wants to sell the girls themselves. That's when the big deals start to happen. He sets up the house on Prescott, starts asking half a million per girl."

"Half a mil?"

"At least. These girls are *owned*, one man to a girl. Akakievich offers home delivery, sends them in a car."

Jack ashes his cigarette against the rail of the balcony and grinds it out. He's suddenly not interested in smoking.

"Why would you want to own someone?"

She shrugs. "How do we know what goes through these bastards' minds? This is the sequence of events—that's all I can give you. The demand gets so big, money can't get you in. It's not enough. Soon it's the city's power: people who can give Akakievich something he can't buy with money. People who can give him protection. Like Clarence."

"I knew about cops. O'Malley? *Definitely*. Just someone Akakievich paid to look the other way. But the fact that it goes all the way up to Clarence?"

She nods. "That's what I've been waiting to get proof of. Now Freeman says it goes further."

Jack shakes his head. What else can he do? "When Akakievich has Clarence, what's he need a small-time vice cop for?"

"Exactly. I'm thinking Clarence needed O'Malley to make it look like something was being done. But it wasn't."

She holds up her hand, first finger extended.

"And this is where it gets real pretty. The next service Alexi starts charging for is anonymity: the assurance that no one can get his client list. *This* becomes the premier service, where the real money comes from. These guys want to keep their names secret, he asks them for another half million."

"Are these people insane?"

Gannon looks out over the city, the tall buildings and the city lights all around them in the fog. "They're fucked. They'll give him whatever he wants now. Including a new red-light district all to himself in Mission Bay. That, Jack, *that's* what this is all about. It's about getting the names on that list and stopping Akakievich."

"Clarence isn't enough?" Jack says. "You're going after them all."

She nods. "Clean up the city. *That's* what the U.S. government is paying me to do."

"That's what O'Malley would've given you."

She shakes her head. "O'Malley wouldn't have known about everyone. Still, he'd have been a start. He could have given us more than Clarence, I'm guessing. And we could have used his testimony in front of a grand jury."

"That was O'Malley's private girl in the back of his car?"

She nods. "His message that he'd become expendable."

"But what about the other girl? The one in the Chevy."

"That we don't know. That's why Akakievich has to go down fast."

Jack looks out over the city skyline through the fog. The buildings around him hold hundreds of fancy apartments; in their windows he can see flat-screen TVs, beautiful furniture, tasteful lighting. New buildings are coming up close to the bridge; streets of row houses stretch north toward the Bay. The city's growing, expanding, getting bigger and richer every year.

"Motherfucker learned the American way," Jack says.

"Maybe he did." She shrugs, wraps her arms around herself, and shivers a little. "Or maybe he knows he's in the shit. All I know is I want to stop him before he kills any more girls." She turns toward the door and slides it open. "*That* can't stand."

31

Gannon's phone is ringing, and she takes off down the hall to answer it. Jack meets Tom as he's closing the door to their daughter's bedroom.

"You're lucky," Tom says, "most people would have bet on you being dead by now."

"Really?"

He gives a bit of a shrug. "This is serious, Jack. It's a good thing you're taking our protection."

Jack's about to respond, but Gannon comes at them with her phone closed. She grabs her purse off the kitchen counter. "Come on, Jack, we've got a scene in Japantown. It looks like another girl."

"What?" Jack looks back at Tom, unsure why he's going out again into the night. "Shouldn't I stay?"

"No. You come with me. Until this is over, I'm not letting you out of my sight." Gannon puckers an air kiss toward Tom. "Stay with Samantha?"

Tom nods. With a solemn look on his face, he follows them into the kitchen and to the front door. Jack still wants to say something back to him, but Gannon's pulling him out the door by his arm.

***

In the car, Jack braces himself against the dashboard with both arms as Gannon corners hard toward the garage exit, clicking the door opener above her visor.

As the door slides out of the way, Gannon shoots the car out onto the street above and scrapes the rear bumper against the bottom of the ramp. "Shit," she says. "I always do that." She looks back in the rearview mirror, and Jack turns around to see the door sliding closed.

She turns hard again and starts heading west toward Japantown.

As Gannon blasts through a stop sign leaning on her horn, Jack watches a few spectators follow the car with wide eyes. Pretty much anything goes in San Francisco, but someone starts driving around like the chase scene in *Bullet* and it doesn't go unnoticed.

"Don't you have a siren on this thing or something?"

"FBI, Jack. We don't do that." She slows down as they come to a red light and pats Jack on the knee. "It's okay, though." When she sees there's no traffic coming, she drives through the light.

Jack puts on his seatbelt. Not always his first instinct when he gets into a car, but a precaution he's not too big to take when needed.

Gannon blows some hair out of her face and makes a hard right onto Sutter heading west. The traffic's heavier on Sutter, and she slows down. Jack thinks about lighting a cigarette but doesn't want to encourage her. On the other hand, a cigarette on her breath will play a lot better at a crime scene than a good whiff of what she's been drinking.

He takes out his pack. "Smoke?"

"Thanks." She takes one and lets Jack light it for her. When he's got one lit for himself, he lowers the window.

She takes a long drag, squinting her eyes, and then puts her hand back on the wheel like she's been driving and smoking this way all her life.

"All Freeman amounts to is one questionable witness," she says.

"Clarence, then?" When she doesn't answer, Jack smokes his cigarette and waits.

"Yeah. Maybe." Then she shakes her head. "We don't know." She reaches into her purse to get out the BlackBerry. "Here." She hands it to Jack. "Call Shaw."

Jack scrolls through the names on her caller list without recognizing any. Then he gets to Shaw's and calls the man's cell, but Shaw doesn't answer.

"So we've got three dead girls now *and* O'Malley *and* Hopkins. Does that mean Akakievich's big fish start showing up dead next?"

She shakes her head. "Or worse. My bigger fear is they'll give Akakievich what he wants."

32

Gannon flashes her wallet toward the blue suits at the crime scene, and they raise the yellow tape for her. Their main job appears to be holding back the press—a couple of beat reporters and a cameraman snapping shots of the scene. Maybe a dozen other people stand outside the yellow tape, watching the cops do their work. It's the center of Japantown, almost exactly across the street from the restaurant Junius Ponds used to frequent. Behind the scene, the Peace Tower stretches up into the night like an ironic backdrop to the night's events. The girl lies on the pavement, covered by a blanket.

When one of the cops starts to say something to Jack, he nods at the guy—the same one from last night—and tells him the same line: "Forensics." The guy smiles, nods at Jack. He holds up the yellow tape to let him pass.

"How'd you—"

"The cops," Jack says. "They're all big fans of the movie."

Gannon slips a cord out of her wallet and loops it around her neck to keep the badge on her chest. It sits right in the middle of her cleavage, slanting upward.

This time there's no car, only the empty concrete plaza and a handful of police officers standing around talking, a team of guys from the coroner's office already working around the body, surveying the scene. Gannon walks right up to the girl. There's a detective wearing a suit, a nice tie, and when he looks at her, his mouth almost falls open.

"Williams," he says when he's gathered himself. "She's been here less than two hours. Body's just now going cold." He gestures to Jack with his chin. "Who's this?"

"He's with me."

Williams gives Jack a hard look. He knows he's getting dicked around by a Fed and there's nothing he can do about it. Jack gives him his best smile, trying to show the guy they're on the same side. Williams stares at Jack for a heartbeat, then goes back to writing on his pad.

When Gannon lowers the blanket from the girl's face, Jack sees she's older than the others, maybe almost eighteen. The idea that she could be used up, too old for the game, doesn't seem possible. Looking at her face, Jack doesn't see how that could ever be true. She has red hair and a thin chin, skin pale enough to make you believe she spent part of her life underwater. Her head and a beautiful pair of soft shoulders show over the top of the dark SFPD blanket. Gannon lifts it to take a look, and Jack doesn't think twice before he comes around to see more. She's thin, but with a set of some plastic surgeon's finest creations across her chest, swelling out over her arms. Below her thin, flat stomach, a torch of red hair is barely visible in the night.

Gannon lowers the blanket. She goes down to the legs and crouches to get close before lifting the blanket. "No scars," she says.

Williams fills them in. "Cause of death is suffocation.

Someone put a bag over this girl's head and waited for her to die. Contusions on the wrists and ankles. My bet is she was tied down when it happened."

Gannon stands up. "Anyone see anything?"

Williams points his pencil at an elderly Japanese couple sitting on one of the plaza's concrete benches. "They found the body. Didn't see it arrive. Found her here, right where you see. Drop and run."

Gannon nods. The girl's hair is spread out around her face, her lips dark in contrast to the rest of her face.

"She's Russian?" Jack asks.

"No ID yet." Williams keeps writing in his pad, speaks without looking up from his work. "But if I had to guess, I'd say she ran in the same circles with the girl we found at the Embarcadero last night. Same basic setup."

Gannon blows out a hard breath, looking up at the big restaurant across the street, its picture window and the tables on the second floor. "No witnesses."

Williams raises his head. He glances over his shoulder, back toward the street and up at the restaurant. "No one's talking."

33

After convincing Williams to sit on his report, keep the press outside the yellow tape, and not release any information about the girl, especially not any pictures, Gannon leads Jack back to her car, swearing a blue streak all the way.

She's still calm and composed physically, walking with determination, but under her breath, she's letting it all go.

In the car, she starts the engine and takes another cigarette, smokes it with the window open, the engine idling. Jack can feel her frustration across the seat.

"This upsets you."

"I've seen this girl before," she says. "That's the problem."

Jack wants to ask when, or with whom, but he knows she'll tell him when she's ready.

She takes a long drag off the cigarette, one of her own, a Marlboro red, and coughs into the top of her fist. Then she takes out her cell, flips it open, and dials a number.

"Calling Shaw?" Jack asks. He watches two guys from the coroner's office lift the girl's body onto a stretcher.

"Tom," Gannon says. For a moment, Jack thinks she's talking to him, but she's talking into the phone. "It's the redhead."

The coroners stoop to lift the girl, bending at the knees and crouching like they're supposed to. As they start to lift, her blanket begins to fall off. It gets caught by the wind, and Jack catches a glimpse of her legs. The guy by her feet lunges for the blanket, braces his end of the stretcher against a hip, and leans forward to try and keep it on her. But this throws the stretcher off balance, and the girl starts to slide. Her calf falls out first, and then her knee bends.

Gannon says, "The one from my last op. The one from the limo." She pauses. "Right. Right. That's her."

The guy at the girl's head drops his end of the stretcher to catch her body, going for her shoulders, as another gust of foggy air finishes pulling off the blanket. Faced with the choice of saving the blanket or the stretcher or letting the girl's feet fall, the other chooses her feet, and in a moment, the two gray uniforms stand holding a naked girl between them. She collapses at the middle as her body bends into a V.

Jack watches flashes go off all along the line of yellow tape as reporters take shots of the scene: two men from the coroner's office standing and holding opposite ends of a young naked dead girl, her face clearly visible in the tangle of red hair. The men lower her to the ground and scramble to get the blanket over her again.

Gannon is oblivious to all of this; she's facing the other way, looking toward the street as she talks on the phone. Given how pissed off she is, Jack considers this a blessing.

"I'm sure," Gannon says. "The one he said was his daughter's friend."

Jack waits to hear what she says next.

Gannon agrees with Tom on the phone, says something Jack can't understand, and flips the phone closed.

"What is it?" Jack asks. "Who is she?"

Gannon takes a long pull off her Marlboro, ashes it hard against the lip of the car's ashtray. "Here's the thing," she says. "I've been on this case about four months. Four months of following people around, trying to find out as much as I can about Akakievich and his operation. But before that—" She looks at Jack, takes another drag. As she lets it out, she squints, says in a rough voice. "You can't repeat this to anyone, ever."

Jack nods. "Sure."

"Before I was on this, I was on a number of duties, but one night I filled in for a guy who normally works the duty outside the mayor's residence. Since 9/11, don't ask me why and don't get me started on the politics of this, major political figures, like mayors of big cities, get federal escort. Full FBI Homeland Security protection."

"War On Terror," Jack says.

"Right. Exactly. Only thing is, there's no terrorists even thinking about going after Mayor Grant. The only terror he's causing is to the girls he brings home when his wife's not looking." She exhales hard, rests the cigarette in the ashtray. "Anyway, this is the girl I saw. After three a.m., the mayor calls to have his limo brought in, walks this girl out, and lets her into the back." Gannon nods toward the scene next to them, where the two men have finally succeeded in securing the blanket and are starting to lift the girl on the stretcher again. "That's his girl."

Gannon takes the cigarette out of the ashtray, pulls a last drag, and grinds it out among the ashes.

"Shit. Akakievich has the mayor *and* the chief of police sleeping with his girls?"

"Not only that, but he's got balls big enough to go after them."

Jack looks out the window, watches the two coroners finally load the stretcher into the back of a black-and-white van. "This thing's getting bigger and bigger."

"That's part of what scares me," she says.

Jack's not sure if he wants to know the answer to his next question, but he has to ask. "What's the other part?"

"It's that either Akakievich must be close to taking over this city, or Freeman was right about him hurting more of these girls."

34

Whether he wants to be in the middle of this for the rest of the night, Jack's not sure, but it's not like he has much choice in the matter. Gannon's got a look on her face like she could bend iron, and she's driving like she means it.

Ahead of them a taxi door opens on the street side, and she leans on the horn, swerves to go around it, and doesn't look back when they're past.

"I'm going to say something now, Jack, that you're not going to like."

"Okay." Jack holds up his hands. Whether she sees him or not, it's his natural show of backing off.

Gannon doesn't look over. She's still driving too fast, her fingers tight on the wheel. "I think we should go after Akakievich now. Call in Shaw, bring the forces down on his house before something happens that we can't tie to the mayor anymore and before someone else gets killed."

"You mean another girl."

"Another girl or the mayor or Clarence or one of *us*."

"Call Shaw," Jack says. "I'm with you."

She nods. "First I have to call Tom." Gannon takes her phone out of her purse, flips it open, and dials by hitting one button.

When Tom answers, she says she's considering taking a look inside Prescott.

Then she starts agreeing a lot, nodding and listening to what Tom's saying on the other end of the phone. Jack wishes she'd put Tom on speaker.

"I don't care if it's Saturday night. Tell them that the girl who just got hit is connected to Mayor Grant and that Chief Clarence is involved in this."

When the light turns to green, Gannon crosses the intersection and pulls over, double-parks the car, her hazards blinking. She's listening again. "I hear you," she says finally, "but this whole thing's going to blow up in our faces if we don't see what we can find."

Then she's quiet again, listening. "Okay," she says. She hangs up.

"What?"

"He's not in love with the idea—"

"Let's call Shaw, see where he is."

"—but I convinced him to call in to our superiors and ask for the green light on a visit. He's doubtful, but he's working on a third opinion."

"Call Shaw. He might—"

She nods; she's already dialing, saying Shaw's name into the phone and asking him where he is, what he's turned up in North Beach.

Jack looks out the window, up at some apartment buildings. They're all painted white with security grates in front of the doorways. On the other side of the street is a big industrial building.

"I know," Gannon says. "And I don't care if we have to go in by ourselves."

"I want to go in too," Jack says.

"Okay," she says after a while.

Jack's not sure she heard him. "I want to go in," he says.

Gannon agrees to something Shaw says on the other end. Then she's listening again.

"Good," she says. "We're there in ten." She hangs up.

"I'm going in if you are," Jack says.

"I heard you." She puts the car in drive and pulls out across two lanes with just a quick glance behind her to make sure it's clear. At the end of the block, she turns north, away from her building toward North Beach.

Her phone rings, and she flips it open one-handed, spits her last name into the mouthpiece.

"It's me," Tom says. Now he's on speaker. "We have a problem."

"Dockery," she says.

"This is you getting pulled back from up above. We don't have the authorization to go into the house on Prescott yet. They think if we go in now, we won't find enough to break this up. Maybe we'll get some of Akakievich's goons, but we're not going to get Alexi and we're not going to get his list of customers."

Gannon shakes her head; Jack's starting to like her more and more every minute. "No," she says. "We go in now, we clean this up and let the customers walk. They will anyway. We need to stop this before any more of these girls get killed. *They're* the biggest victims in this whole thing. They—"

"Jane."

There's silence on the other end of the phone, a silence Jack doesn't like. Gannon slows down, moves to the right lane, and parks the car against the curb.

"Janey," Tom says. "You're called off."

She shakes her head and then squeezes the bridge of her nose between her thumb and two fingers. "Okay, Tom. I hear you."

"Good, Jane. Why don't you come home? Bring Palms in, and we'll call it a night."

"Okay."

"Good thinking, soldier," he says. "I know this isn't an easy call."

She flips the phone closed.

"What is this?" Jack asks.

"I don't know." Gannon rests her forehead against the steering wheel. "But it fucking sucks."

35

The car's gotten warm, and Jack reaches to turn down the heater, then changes his mind and opens the window. He takes a cigarette out of his pack and lights it, then blows the first drag out into the night. It's cold outside, the usual severe drop in temperature after the sun goes down, even more so when a fog's rolled in for the night like it has. Moisture has condensed on the windows of the parked car next to them.

"Cold night," Jack says. The dashboard clock reads ten-thirty.

Gannon sits up. She starts to say something about having a drag or a cigarette of her own, but stops midsentence and drops her hands into her lap. Her purse with the phone in it drops to the floor.

"What's next?" Jack asks.

"I go to sleep. Live to fight another day. Maybe let the mayor walk his way out of this mess."

The thought of sleeping on her couch or in a guest bedroom in that condo strikes Jack as less than appealing. Much less. He doesn't want to be anyone else's responsibility or need someone watching his ass. And the last thing he wants, really, is to back off Akakievich now.

With Shaw in North Beach already, heading to Prescott, Jack wants to be there; he wants to be in on what happens tonight. At least that's what he thinks as he looks up at a tall, dark building, takes a long drag, and feels the calming warmth flow into his lungs. As he looks up to the building's top, he sees it's the former Bank of America Building with jagged edges along the top, where the sniper fired from in the opening scene of *Dirty Harry*.

"Maybe," Gannon says finally, "there's another option for you." She looks around and then shifts into drive, starts moving slowly again.

Jack thinks about Dirty Harry, Sergeant Mike Haggerty, and what those guys would do in a situation like this. Maybe Shaw's more like them than Jack knows. He wants to be around to see. *He* wants to be like these characters.

"Sometimes this job doesn't make any sense, Jack. You think you're going after one thing and then you're not. Or you're told that you can't. It's enough to piss a woman off, you know? But you know what?"

"What?"

"You can go in. I turn you over to Shaw's custody, and then it's you two." Gannon's expression hasn't changed: She's focused on the road, facing straight ahead.

"Okay," he says. "I'm up for that."

She smiles. "Good."

That's when the phone beeps, like walkie-talkie phones do, and then Shaw's unmistakable voice comes out of Gannon's purse. "Jane." She starts to pick up the purse, and Shaw says her first name again.

When she gets the purse, the phone beeps. "I'm here,"

SETH HARWOOD

Gannon says. She raises her eyebrows. "Shaw, I got called off. No Feds."

Jack takes a last drag of his cigarette and flicks the butt out toward the curb. He knows it's a bad habit but doesn't want to start fixing his habits tonight. "Tell Shaw I know how we can get inside," Jack says. "Tell him I'll meet him in North Beach in ten minutes at the corner of Broadway and Columbus."

"Jack says—" Gannon stops. She holds the phone away from her face and looks at Jack.

"You go home. Be with Tom, follow your orders."

She brings the phone back to her mouth.

Truth is, all Jack knows in North Beach is the café and the house on Prescott. But he wants to be on his own again and working the night like he was before she picked him up. Sure, Freeman's gone and this is dangerous, but Jack likes his chances with the cop from Walnut Creek, the only other outsider in all this.

He needs to play this role, the only one he has.

36

In North Beach the streets are full of life; crowds of people wait outside the clubs and well-dressed twenty-somethings patrol for possible hookups.

"Wait," Jack says. "Stop here. I see someone I know."

He sees the bouncer at the club with the blue neon sign, the script he still can't read. He's spoken to this guy for less than five minutes, but it's an opportunity to get away from the Feds and provide Gannon with an excuse or a good story to explain his absence.

"Who?"

"Stop for a minute. I see a guy who might know something."

Gannon brings the car to a stop at the corner where Kearny and Columbus meet at an angle, the club walls coming to a point—like the Flatiron building in New York, but much smaller.

The end of the line to the club is right outside Jack's door.

"I need to do this," he says. "Just like you need to follow your orders to go home."

She nods, but barely.

As Jack's getting out of the car, Gannon calls him back. "Jack," she says. She leans across the seat to look him straight in the eye, a gold cross hanging from a chain around her neck. "Be careful."

Jack winks. "That's the only way to be."

"No, Jack," she says. She reaches across the front seat and grabs his hand. "Be *careful*. And get that fucker who's killing these girls."

He nods. "I will."

At the front of the line, he clasps hands with the same flat-topped bouncer, and the guy seems happy to have Jack come back. "Nice cut," he says, nodding toward Jack's head.

Jack runs his hand over the new buzz, thanks the guy. In the line, a woman in a tight red dress says something to the guy she's with, pointing at Jack with her pinky, trying not to make it too obvious.

"I need a favor," Jack tells the bouncer.

"Put me in a movie and I'll give you anything you need." The guy laughs, either partly embarrassed about the pitch or because it's an actual joke. Jack's not sure which.

He nods, agrees to find the guy a spot in his next movie, but doesn't tell the guy he isn't sure that'll ever happen. "I need to get in," Jack says.

"Shit. That all?" The guy starts to unlatch the red rope. "If that was it, you should've just asked. No problem."

Jack thanks the guy and gives him a touch on the shoulder as he walks onto the black carpet and under the entranceway heater. He glances back toward the end of the line to where Gannon parked her car. She's already gone.

***

On the dance floor, Jack makes his way through the crowd slowly, trying to squeeze through the couples and small groups, the guys pressing their asses into women. The music comes strong out of the DJ booth at the back of the big room and from speakers all around. It's reggae: hard lyrics with a beat strong enough to make the whole crowd move in one motion, people nodding their heads and bending their knees as one. Halfway across the floor, Jack makes eye contact with a beautiful brunette. She's dancing with a big bodybuilder type, and she smiles wide at Jack as she presses her ass up into the guy's crotch. Then she squeezes her lips together in a kissing motion, her lipstick shining and her eyes closing for a moment. Jack makes sure he's not still looking when her eyes open.

At the bar, he squeezes in between a few other clubbers and puts down a twenty. "Give me a bottled water," he says. "And tell me if this place has a back exit."

The bartender pulls the water out of a cooler behind the counter, flips it once, and sets it down onto the bar. Jack keeps his hand on the twenty as the bartender reaches for it. She's tough-looking, a young Asian American woman with nice arms and a kind face.

"How can I get out the back door of this place?"

"Jack Palms?"

He nods, laughs to himself because getting recognized like this still strikes him as funny. "Yeah. Help me out?"

"Come on." She lets go of the twenty and walks to the side of the bar. There she ducks under it and gets out from behind. Jack takes longer to get around the people and through the groups, but he gets to her, and she takes his hand, leads him toward the back of the room.

Her hand is cool and maybe a little wet; she's been handling cold drinks. But there's something nice about the touch of someone else's hand, about being pulled along like this by a good-looking woman. She leads him to a black wall and to a black door he'd never have noticed, and unlocks it by entering a code.

As the door opens, Jack hesitates for a moment, and so does she.

She looks up at him, still holding his hand, and he offers her the twenty. She shakes her head. "No thanks. Can I have one kiss from the movie star?"

Jack laughs again. "Sure."

She stretches up onto her toes, and Jack bends down. He kisses her—what else is he supposed to do?—and then he feels her hand on the back of his head and it becomes a long kiss: soft at first with a few gentle puckers as their lips get to know each other and then harder and wet. Jack takes her middle in an arm. She smells like candy: some sort of sweet smell. What is it with him and bartenders, he wonders.

And then, as fast as it started, it's over. She licks his upper lip once and lowers her face away from his. She's smiling, and Jack can feel a smile on his face too. Outside it's cold and the cold is blowing into the club, moist and breezy like the city.

"Thanks?" Jack says.

She shakes her head, pushes the hand with the twenty back toward his pocket.

"See you around," she tells him, and then she turns and walks back toward the bar.

Jack stands in the doorway, watching her blend back into the crowd. "Okay," he says, and he ducks outside. When the door closes, he sees he's back on Columbus. He starts to head away from Broadway and pulls out his phone.

"What the fuck *was* that?" He has to ask it, even if there's no one to listen. He shakes it off; there's work to do tonight, and he's got to catch up with Shaw.

Jack finds Shaw's card in his pocket, fishes it out, and looks at the back. It's still the same: a cell-phone number written in Mills Hopkins's hand. Jack flips open his phone and punches in the numbers, then waits, listening to it ring as he crosses the street and turns onto a side street heading toward the Bay. Away from Columbus, the streets are quiet, darker.

Shaw answers the phone, more bark than greeting.

"Yeah. It's Palms."

Shaw speaks fast. "Palms, where you at? I'm here waiting. Broadway and Columbus."

Jack turns again, heads up toward Broadway.

"Too bright there. Can you meet me on Broadway and—" Jack remembers a small street right across from the Pretty Lady. "Rowland?" It's his best guess at remembering the street name.

"Yeah. I can get there. What about Gannon?"

"She'll act pissed, say I ducked her, but she knows this is how it needs to be."

"Do *you?*"

"Give me one hour, Shaw. We check out Prescott for that long, and then we see."

There's a pause on Shaw's end. All Jack hears is his own footsteps.

"Okay," Shaw says. "One hour: That's how long you have to show me what the fuck we can do."

Part III

Into the night

37

As Jack walks, he stays ready to duck into an alley or between two cars if he spots anyone who looks like either of the two Russian Suits. It's mostly people out for the night, wearing flashy clothes and noticeably buzzing, so suits like the Russians wear stick out. He watches for Gannon too, any car that looks like her big American Town Car, just in case she changed her mind.

With the phone back in his pocket, turned off, he zips up his leather jacket for warmth, digs his hands into the pockets. He tells himself that he's okay, that he made a good move losing Gannon. Shaw will either help him out, take him back to her, or let him go. If it's the last, Jack's not sure where he'll head, but he can figure that out when it happens. No going back now.

The streets get brighter as he nears Broadway. Broadway itself is lit up like day with the extra large strip-joint signs and the overhead streetlights. At least the city planners know what streets to keep honest—though if they really gave a shit, they'd put a spotlight over the Tenderloin.

Jack ducks into an empty doorway where he can see the Pretty Lady and Broadway up toward Columbus without being seen. It's a residential building, one where no one's bothered to change the burned-out lightbulb over the entrance. Here in the shadows, he takes out his pack and lights up.

Something about the fog and the cold makes a cigarette nicer, a pleasure you don't find smoking in the summer when it's hot, hot like it gets down in LA or back on the East Coast. Here, even in the summer, you can count on a good chill rolling in every night—sometimes all day. Jack lets it embrace him as he takes the first solid drag.

Outside the Pretty Lady, the same two bouncers stand talking. Jack wonders if Freeman's old pals know he got shot, how they'd react if they knew Jack pulled the trigger. He's been trying to get that whole scene at the hotel out of his mind, push it away and pretend like it never happened. Jack takes a deep drag, considers whether he wants this, how it feels to be in his body in this world.

He takes stock. It's the same him: the same leather jacket against his arms, the same skin feeling the cold, the same face that he knows needs a shave, the same hair now that he's had a cut and lost his highway craziness. He looks down and sees his feet, feels them on the ground, holding his weight. Sure he could use a few trips to the gym, and he needs to stretch, loosen up, and start caring for his body again. But it's him. Even the stiffness feels familiar.

He pushes the image of Freeman's bloody hand, the big man squeezing his whole face in rage, out of his thoughts. He tries to concentrate on the street in front of him.

That's when he sees Shaw. The cop has on a dark leather jacket—shiny, tight, not like Jack's. It has nothing to do with a motorcycle at all. He wears a tight black beanie pulled down to his eyebrows. With his hands in his pockets, he could be anyone.

Here in San Francisco, twenty miles or more from Walnut Creek, he might as well be. And that's what Jack needs, what he hopes will get them through.

When Jack sees that it's clear, that Shaw's alone, he drops his cigarette to the stoop and grinds it under his toe. He steps from the door frame and into the thin light of Rowland.

The cop recognizes Jack, gives the upward nod and starts coming toward him.

"This better be good, Palms." He comes up to Jack, stands close enough that he could hit him. "I get caught in some shit, that's not good."

"Maybe we're better off without the Feds right now," Jack says. "Maybe Gannon even knows it. You see any other choices?"

"I go in myself. Or I go home and call it a night." Shaw sticks a gloved finger into Jack's chest. "I'm not sure you know what you're doing."

Jack knocks Shaw's hand away. The two stare at each other for a long moment, then the cop nods. "Okay. But I'm not saying we go into that house just the two of us. I'm not saying I agree with that."

"Not yet," Jack says. "Come on."

Jack starts walking up Broadway, toward the Bay, keeping an eye out for the Russians. He stays across the street from the Pretty Lady, doesn't make eye contact with the bouncers outside. From there, he follows the same path he took the other night, back when they told him how to get to Tedeschi's Café.

Shaw says, "This whole area was O'Malley's stakeout. This is Akakievich's hood."

"Then we're in the right place. Keep your eyes open. If you

see any nice cars, try to pick out who's in them. Maybe we can find out who's buying these girls."

Shaw nods. "Okay, Jack. It'll be that easy."

They walk for a few steps and reach the corner of Bartol. Jack looks up the dark, narrow block and sees the café, the same Russian sitting at one of the outside tables under a single light, reading a newspaper. "That's the place," Jack says. "And that's our guy."

"Right."

"You want into the Top Notch, you go there, buy a dessert, and they give you the code. A password. That's what Freeman did the other night."

"Yeah? So what's your idea?"

Jack walks back around the corner. Broadway's noticeably brighter but still quiet, a few cars going up and down and not much foot traffic. Jack doesn't see any snipers waiting in lit windows, no eyes following their moves. But that doesn't mean no one's watching.

He's doing what Mike Haggerty would've done in *Shake 'Em Down*. Sometimes people don't expect you to try the most obvious approach—the front door. That's what he's banking on.

That, and maybe a little of him is starting to feel like old Mike. He's got blood on his hands now; he's in this new world.

"Palms."

Jack snaps back to see Shaw looking at him, waiting for an answer.

"I've got two thoughts: Either we go take that motherfucker and break him down in an alley, hold a gun to his head and make him tell us everything he knows. That's the easy method."

"Fuck." Shaw spits on the sidewalk. "What's the hard?"

"The hard is you go up and pretend you're just some dude, tell him you heard about this place, try to get him to let you get the password. Then we both bust into the house when they open the door, and we try to find out what's what."

"Nice," Shaw says, already shaking his head. He puts a firm hand on Jack's shoulder to make sure he's listening. "Let's entertain the thought for a minute that in fact the mayor is involved. You know how cocky Akakievich would have to be to try to start that war?" Shaw shakes his head. "We assume he's been working under some sanction, some look-the-other-way shit. Now he's ready to drop that and take on the city. You really want to take that on?"

Jack chews his lip. He's been hearing this shit since he teamed up with Freeman. People telling him this thing's too big for him. The only one who hasn't given it to him is Jane Gannon, the only one he's not sure he can trust. And just like that, Jack sees it all turn around on him, sees maybe all his assumptions could be wrong. But if Shaw's a dirty cop too and this whole thing extends clear to Walnut Creek, he might as well go straight to Akakievich now. Because there's no fucking way he'll be able to run.

"Yeah," Jack says. "Not only do I want to be here right now, but that war is what I'm counting on."

38

Jack can feel his heart beat in his chest, his blood moving faster. Both men have their hands by their sides, like old gunfighters daring each other to draw. If Shaw takes a swing, Jack's ready for it.

"You have a gun?" Shaw asks.

Jack shakes his head. "No. But I'll bet you good money that guy with the newspaper does."

"So?"

"So you get the drop on him and hold your gun to his head, we have two guns."

Shaw meets Jack's eyes and neither of them blinks. Then Shaw laughs, spits on the sidewalk less than six inches from Jack's shoe. "You better hope he's packing something special. Because it's going to take an automatic to get our asses into that house."

Shaw starts toward the corner of Bartol, looking around the edge. When he can see the guard, he moves out of sight. "We get the drop on that dude and just talk to him. See what we can find out."

Jack stands in the open. If the guard turned around, away from his newspaper, he'd see Jack, and Jack doesn't care.

Shaw pulls him back. "*You* follow *me*," he says.

"Be my guest." Jack gestures toward the guard.

"Fuck you, Palms." Shaw slaps him lightly on the side of the face—maybe it feels good to get that out of the way—and takes two steps around the corner, looks at where he's headed, and walks straight for the café.

As Shaw walks up the alley—the café is in the middle of the block—Jack watches him go. He doesn't want to advertise that Shaw's not alone. But he doesn't want Shaw to be alone either.

Jack starts up the opposite side, mirroring Shaw. When the cop gets close enough to the café that the guard sees him, the guy stops reading and puts down his newspaper. Jack watches as the guard takes a cigarette out of a pack on the table and flips it in the air, catching the filter between his lips. A nice trick. He lifts his lighter as Shaw gets close, but the other hand drops down out of sight.

If this guy's worth his vodka, he can probably peg Shaw as a cop from a block away. But maybe that's not bad; maybe enough cops come by for the password that it doesn't raise suspicions anymore.

The guard lights his cigarette one-handed.

Jack angles his face toward the wall to light a cigarette of his own.

As Shaw speaks, the guard blows smoke into his face. Shaw keeps talking, gesturing with his hands and, Jack guesses, going too fast. Then again, why not give Officer Shaw the benefit of the doubt?

Jack glances back up toward the top of the alley. There's nothing there, but his mind's starting to play that trick, making him think he saw something.

The guard says something, and Shaw nods. He puts his hands back into his pockets and heads inside the café. This is where he'll either get what they need or he won't. And Jack's not much on waiting to find out.

"Shit," Jack says, dropping his cigarette onto the sidewalk and heading across to the café.

When the guard sees Jack, he stands, starts shaking his head. He takes a long drag then puts his cigarette into his ashtray. Jack's about five feet away, coming across the little alley right in the middle. There's no turning back now. The guard starts cracking every knuckle he has, wringing his hands like he wants to break every bone in Jack's body. He waits on the sidewalk.

Behind the guard, Shaw turns away from the register. His face goes a shade lighter. Jack sees him mouth the one word he doesn't want to see: "No."

The Russian's big across the chest but he has a spare tire that could fit on an Indy 500 race car. He starts to nod at Jack, says his name out loud.

"Yeah, buddy," Jack says, unzipping his jacket for ease of movement. If it comes to it, he's ready to go, to do whatever he can to this dude. Inside the café, a pair of coffee-sipping old men stand up to see what's about to happen.

As Jack moves onto the curb, the guard closes on him and throws a big sweeping haymaker that Jack can see coming two seconds away. He ducks the punch and hits the Russian in the gut with a right, putting everything he has into it, getting him just under the ribs. The guard doubles over and steps away from the parked cars. Jack follows. He throws a left uppercut, a punch he's not used to throwing, that only grazes the Russian's chin and connects more with his cheek. That sets up the guard for a takedown, some kind of move Jack thinks about instead of acts on, and in that moment of indecision, the guard comes at him with a left that Jack barely manages to step away from, then a right that catches him in his ribs.

Jack steps into the table, the wind knocked out of him, and the Russian comes at him hard, angry, and big. He scoops Jack up with both arms, by the shoulder and between the legs, and throws Jack onto the sidewalk. Jack never would have thought the guy had a move that fast in him, but then what's he know about this guy—any of this, really?

When the guard gets close enough to follow up, Jack hears Shaw's voice: "Stand still or I send your brains back to the tundra."

"Nice," Jack says, raising himself up to sitting and then pulling himself up with the table. The guard backs away from Jack and raises his hands, but Shaw closes on him fast and hits him square in the face with the butt of his gun, right across the bridge of his nose. A sound of something breaking comes from the guy's face, and he doubles over fast, his hands covering his nose. Shaw presses the gun's barrel against the big thug's temple.

Inside the café, the two old men draw handguns and move toward the door. In the second their move affords him, Jack jumps on the big Russian from the side, taking him down, and yells to Shaw the word "café," which gets Shaw down and moving. He rolls across the ground, comes up prone, and, seeing two guys pointing guns, opens up—shooting through the glass and wood of the door. The first guy jumps back hard and fast, caught in the chest by Shaw's first shots, and the second ducks behind the wooden door frame.

"Oh, fuck," Jack says, aware it's not helpful at a time like this. But what can he do? It comes out.

No going back now. It's on.

Jack takes the guard's head and plants his face into the asphalt. The guy makes a muffled, gurgled scream—something you wouldn't expect to hear except from someone with a broken nose—and brings his hands up to his face. Easy to see how this works. Jack makes a mental note to break big guys' noses more often.

Shaw rolls again and comes up onto one knee, takes a few more shots at the front of the café, close to where the guy last was. The guy comes out of the other side of the door frame, and he shoots through the window, shatters it on his first shot, and Jack puts his head down. He's still on top of the Russian, and he hopes that doesn't make him the first hit.

Shaw fires again, and this time a scream comes from inside the café. Jack can't see anyone. The girl must be crouched behind the counter, and the man's out of sight.

"You hit him?"

Shaw shakes his head. "Can't tell. I made contact, but I think I just clipped him."

The big guard starts to push himself up, and Jack wrenches both of his arms behind his back in a tight lock. He puts all his weight down in the middle of the guy's back.

"You got that one under control?"

"Yeah." Jack twists an arm and the Russian grunts. "He's not going anywhere."

39

"Hold that fucker, Jack."

Shaw starts a low crawl toward the café. That's when Jack notices headlights turning into the alley at its bottom end, filling the narrow opening between the buildings. He strains to look up—more from instinct than thought—and in that moment, the Russian thrusts his head back hard and high enough to catch Jack in the jaw and knock him off. With his arms free, the Russian rolls Jack to the side and, getting up, pushes him away. As Jack scrambles onto all fours, the Russian reaches inside his jacket with one hand.

Jack pounces on him, knocking him back onto the sidewalk, and head-butts him in the face, He follows it up with a right to the stomach, and the Russian squeezes his eyes. Jack knows this guy's developed a major-league pain button right in the center of his face.

A shot comes out of the café—Jack can see the older man shooting from around the side, through the window—and Shaw stands up and rushes the building. He times his leap and flies through the air in front of the window, emptying his clip into the old man. When Shaw hits the ground, he rolls and comes up next to the guard's head. Faster than Jack can move, Shaw reaches inside the guy's jacket and comes out with the gun: a small automatic that looks like a Glock but probably isn't. Shaw trains the second gun on the old man, who slumps to his knees, then falls quietly into what's left of the glass in the windows, the shards cutting his face open from his temple to the other side of his nose.

Jack looks away in time to see the passing car: a silver PT Cruiser, moving slowly. Not Gannon, not any Russian thugs, some poor dumb fuck who turned onto the wrong little excuse for a street. Shaw turns the guard's gun around and hands it to Jack.

"This a Beretta. Try that for feel."

Jack grips the gun and it feels good in his hand, better than a Glock. It's bigger, and the handle doesn't cut off partway down his palm. It just *feels good*. He drops the barrel into the middle of the big guard's face.

"You got something else on you, right?" Jack asks. "Tell me you didn't come all the way to San Francisco with just a couple of clips."

Shaw drops the clip out of his own weapon and inserts a fresh one from inside his jacket. "I got a few more clips, and if I need another piece, I've got two dead assholes inside who won't be using theirs."

Jack taps the big guard lightly on the nose with the Beretta. "You want to talk with us?"

"Fuck you," he says through the blood in his mouth.

"Nice. That's real nice." Jack pushes harder on the guy's nose, causing him to grit his teeth and make a soft whine in the back of his throat. "How's that help your participation?"

At the bottom of the alley, a black sedan's brakes screech as it makes a hard turn, narrowly avoids hitting either curb, and tears down the block. Jack can see it bearing down, and then Shaw's on his feet, firing.

"Jesus," Jack says. The sedan stops. A Ford. He can't see through its tinted windows, but he hears a door open on the other side, and then a second.

Shaw fires twice and jumps forward, hunches against a Mercedes E-Class parked on the curb. Two shots come from the street and disappear into the café. A third breaks the back window of the Mercedes, and Shaw drops down lower as bullets shatter the side windows of the car. Jack slides around so he's facing the street, his body shielded by the bulk of the Russian. He still holds the gun to the guy's temple, and the Russian doesn't move. Shaw rolls, comes out of it shooting from behind the trunk of the Mercedes. Someone in the street yells, and there's another gunshot. Shaw stays where he is, his head up, both arms across the trunk.

"Fuck, fuck, fuck," Jack says under his breath. He doesn't like the situation, the shooting, the holding a gun to a guy's head. This is all getting out of control. "Do *not* move," he tells the guard.

Then Shaw fires two shots into the street, someone else calls out in Russian, and Jack sees a guy from the sedan, medium height, brown haired with a snap-front cap pulled low, duck around the front of the Ford. The guy has on a tan jacket and brown pants. His cap blocks his peripheral vision, and he's focused on Shaw's position as he eases around the front of the car.

Holding the guard's head on the ground with one hand, Jack raises the Beretta.

Still firing at the back end of the Ford, Shaw doesn't see Cap. He crouches behind the Mercedes to reload. It's then that Cap comes around to see Shaw and raises his weapon. But he sees Jack too, and Jack's Beretta. With the gun in his hand and his pick between Shaw and Jack, he freezes for an instant, and Jack fires.

Jack has no other choice, but before this thought has even cleared his processors, he's pulled the trigger, knocked the guy back by his left shoulder onto the hood of the car. Then, as the guy starts to raise his gun, Jack follows the first shot with a second to the center of the chest.

The guy flips back onto the hood and slides down its front, drops into a sitting position on the ground, his legs tangled under him and both hands by his sides. He closes his eyes, swallows hard. When he opens them, he takes a breath and coughs, blood rolling out of his mouth and onto his chin. He's looking at Jack, and a wave of understanding passes across the guy's face. It's the understanding that Jack will be the last person he sees.

"Fuck," Jack says and turns away. He puts his head down, trying to erase Cap's expression from his mind's eye. Luckily, it works—for now.

40

Shaw yells something Jack doesn't understand. The cop rushes out into the street, firing his weapon and screaming, letting go with a series of shots.

Jack closes his eyes for a moment. He still sees the guy's face on the back of his eyelids, that look in his eyes. "Fuck," he says.

That's when the big guard lands on top of him, going for Jack's gun. He's got Jack's hand in his and is trying to pry Jack's finger out of the trigger guard. They wrestle over the gun, and it comes down below their shoulders, gets caught between them. Jack tries to knee the guy in his side. That's when the gun goes off. The Russian makes a loud grunt and a huffing comes out of him. Jack sees the top of the guy's head on his chest and then Shaw above him, rolling the guy off.

Jack gets up into a crouch. The Russian holds his side, breathing with a soft whistle in the back of his throat. "You fucking bastard," he whispers.

Jack looks down at his hands and the gun: There's blood on both, enough that Jack drops the weapon. "Fuck," he says. He wipes his hands on his pants, but that doesn't help, only smears the blood across his legs.

From above him comes Shaw's voice: clear and steady. "Pick

up the gun, Jack." The cop has his foot on the guard's shoulder, aiming his gun at the guy's face. He looks like nothing's happened, like he's only gotten a bit madder.

"Right," Jack says. He takes the gun and stands up. In the street, the black Ford has Jack's friend, Cap, sitting in front of it, and another dead Russian lies splayed out against its trunk. From the silence around them, Jack would guess that another man is dead on the opposite side of the car.

Cap sits wheezing loud enough that Jack can hear it from where he is. His mouth opens and closes on its own, his eyes empty. The blood continues to dribble down his chin. Then Shaw raises his weapon and puts Cap down with a shot to the forehead that echoes in the narrow alley like none of the other shots Jack's heard.

He breathes twice, listening to the shot's reverberations, looking at what he's—*they've*—done. Five dead and the big guard wheezing and trying to hold in the blood seeping out of a fresh hole in his side.

"You want to talk now?" Shaw says to him.

The guard doesn't even acknowledge this. His breathing comes in whistles. "Jack," Shaw says. "Check inside for the girl."

Then a few moments later, "Jack. Check inside."

The hood of the Ford reflects the yellow light from the single streetlight in the middle of the street. Around Jack's feet, glass litters the sidewalk, sparkling as if the street were made of gold.

"You okay, Jack?"

Jack sits back onto his butt, drops his arms down between his legs. Cap wears nice brown shoes, lace-ups shined to perfection, as clean as the Ford's hood.

"Jack. Get the fuck up." Shaw's face comes in front of Jack's, angry now, and the guard's turned his head toward Jack too. "Fuck, Jack. What's wrong with you?"

The lone streetlight glares down. The Ford's side reflects some of that light in a long, thin line along its length. Jack hears his own breath come in and out slowly.

"Jack!" Shaw slaps him.

Mike Haggerty wouldn't do this, wouldn't sit down in the middle of a scene, stop to freak out over a thug he'd killed. He wouldn't even think that guy was a person. "Fuck. Kill or be killed." That was the line Haggerty had uttered when asked how he could sleep at night. Jack had always thought it was bullshit—until tonight.

41

"Jack."

Somewhere there's got to be a cop car on the way, maybe even Agent Gannon rushing to the scene. Haggerty would push through this, stand by Shaw's side.

"I'm okay," Jack says.

"Then get the fuck up off the ground and go inside the café to find that girl working the register."

Jack slowly starts to his feet, climbing to a knee and then rising. The Russian on the ground is breathing with more difficulty now, a vein sticking out on his forehead. Jack puts his hands on his knees and breathes deeply.

"Fuck are you waiting for? Time we got on."

"Right." Jack shakes his head, trying to clear the crap out. He points at the Russian with his gun. "Ask him how we get into the Prescott house."

"You heard the man," Shaw says. "Tell us what we need to know."

The Russian breathes fast and shallow. His face is red. "We'll help you," Jack says. "Tell us what we need and we'll call an ambulance."

"Or don't tell us and I'll fucking pop you," Shaw adds.

Shaw's face is hard, uncompromising. He's sweating, and Jack can see his teeth when he talks.

The Russian tries to speak. The best he can manage is a whisper, and Shaw crouches down to hear it. "Call an ambulance." Shaw waves at Jack. He pushes the gun into the guard's temple. "What else?"

His lips move, and Shaw starts nodding. "That's right. You tell us exactly how we get into that house. What's on the receipt. And what's waiting for us when we get inside." Shaw nods as the guy does his best to keep up with the demands. When he's said enough to make Shaw happy, Shaw pats him on the cheek, tells him help is on the way.

He stands up. "We get that register to print us out a receipt for a crème brûlée, and we take it over to the house. Then we've got to deal with about three heavily armed assholes, and we're in the house, the home base of all this bullshit."

It's either sit and dwell or go all out is the best Jack can see it. Full forward or head home. And he's not ready to go home. "Fuck it," Jack says. "Let's do this."

They head inside the café and find the girl crouched low behind the counter with her hands over her ears, hugging an AK-47 with her elbows and legs. She has her eyes shut but looks up when she hears Shaw say, "Don't shoot." He leans down and takes the assault rifle from her, passes it to Jack. "This might come in handy."

Jack nods. He crouches in front of the girl. "Ring us up for a crème brûlée, okay? You do that and we'll make sure your boyfriend gets out of here alright."

"He is husband," she says. And Jack sees the ring on her

finger: not meager, but not a gigantic rock.

"The police are on their way," Shaw says. "They'll take care of him when they come. But do us a fucking favor and print a receipt for some crème brûlée so we can get on."

He raises his gun, but she waves her hands. "No, no," she says as he pulls her up to her feet. "It is okay," she says. She punches some buttons on the register and hits the big blue button that opens the drawer. A bell goes off, the drawer opens, and she pushes it closed. She hands the just-printed receipt to Shaw. "Here. You have crème brûlée."

Then she sinks back down, returning to her crouch below the counter.

Shaw takes the paper and turns back to the dining area. The two men in there aren't going anywhere. One's covering a table where he fell, and the other's a bloody mess at the window. Blood drips down the wall where his face meets the glass.

Jack steps toward the door with the AK as Shaw checks the old men, takes the guns out of their hands, and shakes the extra bullets out of their pockets. Both guns are snub-nosed revolvers.

"Any gun in a shit storm, right?" Shaw says, pocketing one.

Jack nods. He thinks of Mike Haggerty, tries to channel more of the character's bravado and drive. "You ready to do this?"

"Shit." Shaw looks over his shoulder at Jack as he digs into the bloody man's pockets. "We come this far; I'm not turning back."

"You're out of your jurisdiction, officer."

"Yeah," Shaw says. "And you don't have one. Makes us even, at best." He brings a couple of speedloaders out of the guy's pocket and bounces them in his palm. "Hopkins was a good cop.

This was *his* jurisdiction. We're cleaning up this mess for him."

And Freeman's jurisdiction, Jack wants to say. Part of him misses the big guy. But he's also starting to become fully invested; this is his fight, his beat.

Shaw steps out of the café through what's left of the front door, and Jack follows. He can hear the sirens now, the police cars coming—not close, but definitely not far.

42

Shaw steps to the driver's-side door of the Ford, gets in, guns the engine. "Let's go, Jack. Get your ass in."

The police sirens get louder.

Jack hurries out into the street, past the guard whose ambulance they still haven't called, and lifts Cap's feet to drag him out of the way of the Ford.

"Jack!"

But Jack shakes Shaw off, drags the dead gunman out of the street up onto the curb so they won't have to drive over the body. When that's done, he crosses the alley and comes around to the passenger side of the Ford, where he finds a dark red puddle of blood on the ground but no body. Shaw revs the engine, and Jack gets in, putting the AK between his legs. He pulls the door closed just as Shaw starts to peel out toward the top of the street and Vallejo.

As Shaw makes a hard turn out of the alley, Jack looks at his watch. He doesn't know how much time has passed since Shaw fired his first shot, but he's surprised the police didn't arrive sooner. He asks Shaw for his professional opinion.

"Clarence probably made this a no-fly zone. Wants to let our man Alexi clean up his own shit."

"You think he'd—"

"Shit. Never know what those two had worked out. Alexi's been getting protection. Either that or the FBI spooked the SFPD out of North Beach. Fucking Feds can take over a whole area when they building a case."

Jack realizes most people would pay to have the police show up *faster* when there's a problem. But not sex-trade Russians. Not when they can bring their own heat.

"Prescott," Shaw says.

"A block up and then your first right."

Shaw nods, heads up Vallejo, and then turns onto Akakievich's own private dead end.

"You ever shoot anything like that AK?" Shaw asks.

"Once in target practice and twice with blanks in a movie."

"Well, if you have to shoot it now, these ain't blanks. At least make it *look* good."

"I can use it," Jack says. "It'll look good."

***

Shaw drives halfway down Prescott Court and stops in front of number 32. He leaves the car running and gets out. Jack watches him walk to the sidewalk and start toward the door, no hesitation, no plan.

The street's quiet: no guards that Jack can see and no pedestrians. In most ways it's a perfect location for a prostitution ring: close enough to the strip clubs to be accessible, but not obvious; sheltered enough to be protected, known enough that no one will fuck with you.

Jack gets out on his side of the car. Leaving a car running on the street isn't something he's used to. On the other hand, this car's about as much theirs as the street itself, and probably safer from theft than they'll be from whoever's waiting in that house.

Shaw signals for Jack to hang back. Then, as though they were going through the jungles of Vietnam, he points at his eyes with two fingers, then points at Jack's: Watch me. Definitely some leftover military shit. When Shaw turns back to the house, Jack rests the AK on the Ford's roof, aiming it at the door. Carrying the AK here in the middle of San Francisco feels crazy, like swinging a baseball bat in a supermarket.

Shaw knocks. Jack holds his breath and sights down the barrel of the weapon toward the door. He waits for it to open, ready to take a shot if anything should go wrong. After a little while, he's forced to breathe. He tries to keep it shallow, wanting to hold the gun steady. Then a small slot opens in the door, and Shaw slips the receipt from the café through to whoever's inside.

"Yeah," Jack says, keeping the AK trained on where the door might open. "You go in and we take it, right, buddy?"

Shaw looks around, glances toward Jack, and then, at the sound of a lock sliding open, turns back to the door.

The entranceway to the house becomes visible: There's no one inside, only a vestibule. This is the point at which Jack would like to see Shaw talk his way in, scope out the layout, and then report back—the point at which he'd like them to talk it over and make a plan. But that idea vanishes as Shaw reaches toward the back of his pants and his gun.

"Shit," Jack says. He squints harder and aims the AK, but at what? There's nobody there. For a moment, nothing happens. Shaw checks that his gun is there and then moves forward into the doorway, as if he's a big-money John looking to have a good night. As Shaw goes in, the door starts to close.

"Fuck." Jack takes the AK off the roof.

Shaw knocks his shoulder into the door and pushes it back hard, then grabs it, pulls it toward him, and slams it back into the vestibule wall again. He follows it the second time, drawing his gun and heading into the space created by the door's swing.

In the second this takes, Jack's around the car and running for the stairs, the AK in one hand, his other hand reaching for the Beretta. He hears Shaw fire, sees a flash, and hears somebody yell. That's all Jack hears other than his own feet pounding on the asphalt and the rush of his own breathing.

Ahead of him, the door starts to close, then Shaw stops it. Jack rushes up the steps behind Shaw, pointing the AK and the Beretta around the corner. He's got too much weapon for his hands to handle, but multiple guns make him feel slightly safer. "The fuck are you doing, Jack?"

Shaw lets the door come toward him a little and then slams it all the way open again. This time Jack hears a yell from behind it, a muffled scream like there's someone there, someone Shaw slams into the wall for a third time. Directly in front of Jack, a dead guy sits in a chair, a dark red spot on his forehead and a long black submachine gun across his lap. The blood's starting to flow down his face.

Shaw grabs the Beretta out of Jack's hand, and now he's holding two weapons on the wall behind the door as he kicks it closed. The door swings out to reveal a guard in jeans and a gray sweatshirt holding his nose with one hand. When he sees Shaw's double-fisted gun salutation, he drops his weapon—a short automatic smaller than an Uzi—and raises the other hand.

To the right of the doorway, Jack sees a dark, empty room with a lot of red velvet. There are curtains hanging down the far wall and big armchairs, a fireplace with a big L-shaped couch in front of it. The curtains are a nasty thing to see; Jack knows they can be hiding anything: another entrance, a way to the back rooms, heavy artillery, more guards. "Fuck," he says.

"Run it." Shaw nods at the curtains. "Tear that thing down."

43

Jack looks at Shaw and then back at the curtains. If there's a chance what's back there is going to shoot at him, he's not going to wait. He lets the weapon start its dance, rumbling around in his arms, blasting into the room. Then he holds down the trigger and lets the weapon go full auto, firing and firing, shocking Jack's arms with the repeated kick and recoil. He runs it back and forth across the curtains until no one could be standing behind them. When he lets his finger off the trigger, pieces of the curtains drift through the air; scraps of velvet float to the ground.

"Jack," Shaw says.

He can see a small doorway through the shreds, a gap in the middle of the wall. It's empty. And there was no one hiding behind the curtains—he's glad of that.

"Jack," Shaw says. When Jack looks over, Shaw nods toward the dead guy in the chair. "That is the Kalashnikov AK-74. It's a newer, better version of that AK-47 you just went crazy with."

"Okay."

"Take it," Shaw says. "You spent that whole clip." Jack removes the clip from the AK and releases the round from its chamber as he'd been told to when rehearsing for Haggerty's shooting scenes in the movie. He lowers the gun to the floor and tucks the magazine into a back pocket.

Jack looks down at the bigger gun, its long, curved stock, before he takes it out of the dead man's hands. There's a moment when the guy's fingers hold, but then Jack pulls the gun free.

"Good," Shaw says. "Now say hello to this fuckface right here."

Shaw holds his guns in the face of the guard, tells him to raise both hands. When the hand comes away from his nose, Jack can see a splatter of blood on the guy's face and chest. His nose is a mess, more shattered than broken. He's starting to see how Shaw rolls.

Jack turns his new weapon on the man.

"Watch that other room," Shaw commands. "Anyone comes through that little doorway, you tear them up."

"Unless it's a nice little pretty-looking girl. Right, Officer?"

Shaw grunts.

"Shaw, something tells me you didn't learn this shit in Walnut Creek."

"Shut the fuck up, Jack. Act like you know what you're doing."

Jack steps into the room with the nice furniture and trains his gun on the door, his back to Shaw.

"Where your boys?" Shaw demands of the guard.

"Boys?"

"Your backup! Who's in this place?"

Jack shakes his head, both impressed with and worried by this new side of Shaw. He wishes that he had time to smoke a cigarette, that this night wasn't turning into a cherry-busting party for him: his first kill and his first time shooting real rounds from an automatic weapon.

When the guard speaks again, his accent is thick and Eastern European, a Russian accent Jack's heard enough now to differentiate from the Czech he heard on the road. The guard says something about how he doesn't understand, and Shaw hits him in the nose with one of the guns. Jack hears the sound. The guy doubles over and screams; Shaw hit his button. "Okay. Okay. I will tell."

Out of the corner of his eye, Jack sees Shaw's hand hold the barrel of the gun in the guy's face.

The guard slumps to the ground against the wall and holds his hands above his head. "Please do not to shoot."

And then Jack hears a quiet woman's voice saying something in another language, a sound like Russian. "Hello?" he says.

"You see someone, you shoot," Shaw tells him.

She steps through the doorway and into the room, a tall pale girl of sixteen or seventeen wearing only a lacy black negligee.

"Relax, Alvin," Jack says. "It's just one of the girls."

"You be sure that's all it is, Palms."

Jack goes to the girl. She's thin and pale like the others, but with long, straight blond hair and high cheekbones.

"Hello?" she says when she sees Jack. She tries to force a smile, the look of a girl who's happy to see him, but Jack can see through it. He knows she's scared, a girl too many miles from home, in a city she doesn't know, a house she's probably not allowed to leave except when she's on a call, and he sees the pain in her eyes, pain and maybe a tiny shred of hope that what she's just heard—the shooting and the yelling—means something might be changing, that this night might lead to a better life for her.

Jack holds up his hand for the girl to come no farther. She remains beyond the tattered curtains, her hands above her shoulders, the negligee covering only the very tops of her thighs.

"This is it," the guard says, pointing to his dead friend. "No one but Nathaniel and me." Jack's never heard of a Russian guy named *Nathaniel,* but he's not going to stop this guy's story and ask about that. Nathaniel's dead now anyway.

"We are only ones left. We have small duty."

"Where's Akakievich?"

The guy shakes his head. "He is not here. He leave tonight to Nathaniel and to me. We the watch out now. I am Isaak."

"And?" Shaw raises his voice, losing patience with this guy. "And?"

Jack looks away as he sees Shaw hit the guard again. He hears the sound of a fist hitting raw meat.

Jack takes another look at the girl and lowers his AK; it feels ridiculous to hold a gun like this on a girl. He waves for her to lower her hands, but she won't; she keeps them held high. Jack sees the head of a second girl stick out of a room down the hall behind the blond. She says something to the blond, and in a soft voice, the first girl tells her to wait, says something in Russian that makes the other girl disappear inside. Before she disappears, though, the girl takes one look into the front room, directly at Jack. There's no hope in this girl's face, no fake smile, just fear.

Shaw barks at the guard, "Where's Alexi?"

Isaak frowns; he shakes his head, moving his chin from shoulder to shoulder.

Shaw punches the guard in the face twice, hard. Blood spurts from his nose, even more than before. From outside the house,

Jack hears sirens: police.

"There's no one else here?" Shaw asks.

Isaak shakes his head. "No. It is just me and the girls."

Jack asks, "How many girls?" raising his voice to be heard in the next room.

The guard stops shaking his head. He raises his upper lip, what's left of it, and runs a bloody tongue across the front of his teeth. He finds the gap in the middle of the row, the place where Jack can see Shaw has knocked out or broken a tooth or two. Looking down, he says softly, "There are now only five."

44

"What the fuck?" Shaw says. "You mean all this shit's come down for five girls?"

"There were more. Eight of the most beautiful girls. Now we have less."

Jack whistles. The prices must be as high as he'd been led to believe, the clientele so high-level he's surprised Shaw got in the door.

"This is private club," Isaak continues. "Very exclusive."

The pale blond girl stands with her hands up. There she is: a human being with a definite price. The idea is so pre–Civil War that Jack feels like he's in a time warp. Still, if Gannon was right about San Francisco, if sex slavery is a part of the city, it didn't begin and won't end with Akakievich.

"Whose is she?" Shaw points to the girl.

"No." Isaak shrugs, shakes his head. He makes a clicking sound with his tongue. Jack can't tell whether the noise is intended to mean they're way off, or if it's just a noise this guy's broken mouth makes now. He waves a finger at them, and Jack figures this means the sound was the first. "These girls, even I do not know. Alexi send them out. We do not know."

"Where's your list?"

Isaak shakes his head, a small gesture, his chin barely moving from side to side. "No list. Only Alexi know. Alexi and André."

Jack comes over to the small foyer. "Who killed the other three girls?"

"Killed?" Isaak looks puzzled. "No girls."

"Where did the other three go?"

"Just they leave. Left here."

Jack reaches out to Shaw's arm, lowers the gun. "Relax, big guy. Sounds like we know more about this than he does. Plus, we can show the girls pics to get their Johns later."

At that moment, Jack hears a floorboard creak in the living room near what's left of the curtains; he sees a dark figure as he turns and drops into a crouch with the Kalashnikov pointed into the room. A dark-clothed man stumbles in, a heavy machine gun raised in front of him. He wears a suit, no tie. Beneath his ashen face, his shirt is red with blood, darkest around his left shoulder. The gun's pointed at the front of the house, the covered windows to the right of Jack's position.

"What you want me to do?" Jack asks Shaw. He steadies his crouch, holding the weapon with one knee on the floor and the other knee raised, supporting his elbow. "This guy's in trouble already."

The man makes a noise: not a word, but something Jack hears as an appeal. There's something about his face Jack recognizes, something familiar.

"That's the fuck from the Ford at the café," Shaw says. "I already shot that dude." He raises his gun and shoots him again, hitting the other shoulder. The guy staggers back and keeps his balance like a mummy in an old movie, lowering his gun as he does so. Then, moving slowly, he starts raising the machine gun, lifting the barrel and swinging it toward Jack, his finger on the trigger.

"You've got to be kidding me." Shaw shoots him again, this time in the middle of the chest. The guy wheezes but keeps raising the gun. "Fuck is wrong with this asshole?"

Jack raises the Kalashnikov and aims it right at the guy's face. He looks almost like he's dead already, like there's no point shooting him anymore. But even now, his gray arms keep lifting the machine gun.

"Fuck," Shaw says. "Shoot his ass, Jack. Carve him up!"

Jack holds the Kalashnikov with both hands, sees the guy's face at the other end of the barrel, his eyes practically closed. There's a trickle of blood at his temple.

The guy's less than fifteen feet away. Jack touches the trigger. The cold metal is a foreign feeling, and Jack knows that the last person to touch it is dead now. He sights on the guy's face and sees Freeman's: the look of pain that he had in the hotel and his resigned emptiness at the hospital; Jack sees the face of the Russian he shot outside the café, the last look in his eyes after Jack shot him again; he sees the face of the girl, the blond who's moved to the side of the room now, crouching into the corner with her hands over her face, shaking in fear; and finally he sees the guy, his eyes closed and his face drained of blood.

It's one of the Suits from North Beach that first night, Jack realizes, the ones who tried to rough him up in the alley. This is the guy who first followed Jack, the one with the cell phone. Mr. Gray Suit.

Then his head shoots back at the same time that there is a

loud explosion, and in a blur of red and white, part of his forehead comes apart before Jack's eyes. The guy steps back, then falls down hard on his back, his gun pointed straight up into the air. He starts to fire, riddling the ceiling with bullets, sending white plaster and dust spraying into the room.

Jack closes his eyes, covers his head.

And then the shooting stops. When Jack uncovers his head, smoke fills the room—smoke and plaster dust.

"You freeze up on me like that again, and you'll be the one I shoot." Shaw's voice is cold. Out of the corner of his eye, Jack sees Shaw grab the Russian guard by his shirtfront and hit him hard again in the face with the heel of a gun, the Beretta this time.

"Oh!" The guy shoots both hands to his nose, holding the middle of his face. He starts yelling in Russian, screaming about what Shaw's done.

In the hallway, a big piece of ceiling comes loose and falls onto Gray Suit, breaking in half when it hits him. The guy doesn't move. If he feels anything, this piece of plaster isn't enough to break into his awareness.

Jack looks around. He lowers the automatic rifle.

"You hear me? You want to get us killed?"

Jack thinks back to the guard he shot on the street, how he'd protected Shaw there, but he doesn't say anything. "Yeah," he says. "I hear you. Next time I shoot."

The girl pokes her head up out of her hands and leans forward to see what's left of the guy. She looks concerned, or worse. Jack realizes he wants this to be the start of the end of this life for her, wants her to be able to become something different. But what that is, he has no idea. Maybe she'll wind up in the same state of flux he's in.

Jack stands up and goes over to the body of the Russian. The gun still sticks up in the air, though now the guy's chest and face are obscured by the plaster. Jack pulls at the gun, and for a second it's stuck, then it comes free of the dead man's fingers. He tosses it onto the ground toward the curtain.

The girl says something softly, whispers a name Jack can't make out. Then she looks at Jack. He offers her his hand and helps her to stand up.

She says something else he can't make out and pulls him toward the small opening in the wall.

Jack can't resist following her out of the front room.

"Shaw," he calls back. "This girl's leading me somewhere. I think she wants to show me something."

"Don't go with her, Jack. We've got to get out of here."

But it's too late; the girl's pulling Jack out of the room and into a dark hall. A small red bulb attached to the wall on Jack's right spreads what little light it has to offer.

He wants to go with her and find the rest of these girls, find them and dress them and take them out of here, bring them to a shelter that can offer them some help, *something* that will help them make a new start in this world.

She turns, opens a black door Jack hadn't noticed, and pulls him into a small dark room with dim red lights and taffeta curtains. Here, two girls sit on a bed staring at Jack, both in the same state of undress as the blond. She lets go of Jack's hand and moves toward the wall to a dresser. He looks at the two other girls, tries telling them to stand up.

"We're going to get you out of here," he says. They don't respond. "Help me explain to them," he tells the blond.

He looks at her. She stands against the wall holding a small revolver in both hands, pointing it at Jack.

45

"No," Jack says. He raises his hands and shakes his head in exaggerated motions—anything he can do to let her know he's okay. He takes his hand off the handle of the Kalashnikov, holds it by the barrel as someone might hold a wooden walking stick.

"Palms!" Shaw calls from the front. "Where are you?"

"One minute!"

"Jack. Get your ass back out here."

Jack stays where he is. "We're here to help you." He leans the gun against the wall, holds up both of his hands. "Help," he says. "We help."

The blond holds her gun on Jack. Jack hears a gunshot from the front, then a short scream. The girl looks puzzled—puzzled and concerned.

"You are police?"

This is when Jack starts to feel warm, really warm, and he notices the heater on the other side of the room: one of the electric ones with the bright red elements behind a grill. It makes sense, the girls in negligees like this.

The girl says something Jack doesn't understand. "No," he says, shaking his head again. "It's all going to be okay."

The girls' faces are cold. They look at Jack like he's only the latest in a long line of guards they've seen, guys with guns. They look on edge, frightened from the shots. They know some of the other girls aren't around anymore.

The girl says something else, and from the front of the house, Jack hears a shot. Then another.

"Palms!"

Jack holds his hands up, looks down at the Kalashnikov. "In here," he says.

Shaw knocks the door open and floods the entrance with his body. He holds the Glock pointed at the blond, looks at her and then back out into the hall. "Take the gun from her, Jack."

"What, I—"

"Take the gun, Jack. These girls are more afraid of you than they are of these Russians. They think if they go with you, then anything can happen. If they stay here, at least it's a known."

Another series of shots comes from the front of the house.

"Do it!" Shaw yells. "We're taking them out of here with us!"

Jack crouches as though he's reaching for the Kalashnikov against the wall. The girl doesn't know what to do with her gun now; she's waving it back and forth between Shaw and Jack. Jack makes his move fast: stands and catches the girl at her wrists, pushing the gun up toward the ceiling. She lets go as soon as he gets both hands on the weapon.

"Come on," Shaw says. "Get them out of here and into the hall."

The girls seem to understand. They nod at Jack, and the two on the bed stand up. Jack looks down at the flimsy bedroom slippers on their feet. "Do you three have anything else you can wear?"

More shots come from the front of the house. "Jack. We got to get going. The SF blues are outside in heavy numbers. They're going to surround this place."

Shaw crouches, fires a few shots into the front room.

The blond girl moves toward Jack. His first thought is that she's coming for the gun, but when she moves past him and follows Shaw into the hall, he sees she's got other ideas.

"It will all be okay, ladies," he says, though he's not sure how he'll guarantee that.

He follows Shaw and the girl down the hall, leading the last two girls. "Where are the rest of the women who live here?" he asks one.

She squints up her face, says something Jack can't understand. In the front room, shots riddle the boarded front windows. Shaw is coming back toward Jack in a low crawl.

Jack drops low too; a fresh set of bullets tears through the wood on the far window. Shaw makes it to Jack and comes out of his crawl into a crouch facing back toward the front of the house.

Another set of gunshots comes through the windows, and Jack gets down next to Shaw. "Let's get the fuck out of here," he says.

Shaw looks around them at the cramped hallway.

From outside, the unmistakable squawk of a police bullhorn is followed by a stern cop voice telling them that they should come out with their hands raised, that the police have the house surrounded.

Behind the house there's got to be more houses; there's no way the police can be all the way around. "How'd this fuck get in?" Jack nods toward the corpse under the white chunk of plaster.

"Fuck if I know," Shaw says. "But we better find out, because we're not going out the front. I'm not shooting any cops."

The three girls watch. They're agitated, standing on one foot and then the other. One of them says, "Police? You are not police?"

The blond puts her hand on Jack's wrist.

"No?" she says.

Jack shakes his head. "No. Not police. We want to help you. Help. But first we need to get the fuck out of here."

"Oh," she says. "You *help*?"

Jack nods. "We help. We help *you*."

She starts back into the house, past Shaw and down the hall.

"Actually, I am a cop, in case you've forgotten," Shaw says, but Jack cuts him off.

"Come on."

As the blond goes down the hall, the other girls follow. Jack and Shaw bring up the rear, leaving the gunshots and the commands of the police at their backs. Along the hall are other doors with thin curtains covering them. The doors are very narrow, as if the rooms were designed to be small. Jack opens one to check for other girls, but the room is empty. Just a bed and a small shower in the corner.

"Come on, Jack."

It's warm in the house, warmer as they move down the hall. "Where are the other girls?"

Shaw shrugs. "Not here. We'll have to find out later."

The blond reaches a bookcase at the end of the hall. It's been pushed out from the wall, and she slips behind it, out of sight. The other girls do the same. Shaw looks back, raises his eyebrows at Jack, and follows them.

Jack touches the books and realizes that they're hollow cardboard fronts, that the bookcase is actually the front of a door that's been left open. Behind it, he finds a narrow set of wooden stairs descending into an unfinished basement.

At the front of the house, a cop says through a megaphone that they're ready to start coming inside.

Jack can see one of the girls at the bottom of the stairs, but not the others. He hears something loud slam against the front door of the house, the sound echoing down the hall.

"That's our buddies," Shaw says, already halfway down the creaky stairs. "You coming?"

Jack pulls the bookcase closed. He looks for and finds a handle on the basement side, pulls on it until he hears the door click shut, maybe locking behind them. Then he ducks his head to avoid the low ceiling and the spider webs, and starts down the stairs.

46

The basement is bare except for what you'd expect—a hot water heater, a furnace, a bunch of old furniture. But as the girls walk around to the back of the stairs, the three of them start screaming. Shaw grabs two of them and holds his hands over their mouths. Jack quiets the blond the same way. When he does, he sees what set them off.

A man hangs from a wide pipe that runs along the low basement ceiling, his toes barely touching the ground. Two straps lead up from his shoulders, wrap around the pipe, and tie off. As Jack looks closer, he sees the straps end in rusty metal hooks that go around the man's back and into his shoulders. He can see their pointed tips sticking out in the front. Jack turns the girl away from the sight, back toward the stairs. He can feel her back heaving next to his chest, her sobs. Shaw pushes the other two girls underneath the staircase. They move along its side and to the wall, where a hole leads out of the room. When Jack sees they're gone, he lets the blond go, and she follows them out.

"Wait for us," Jack says.

Above them, something heavy hits the front door again. Jack can tell they're under the front rooms of the house. Soon it'll be flooded with cops who'll find their way down to the basement. "Let's go."

"One second." Shaw walks closer to the hanging man, getting a better look. Jack can see a lot of blood staining what's left of the guy's shirt underneath his arms. The front of the shirt is torn open, revealing a tanned, hairless chest. The guy looks like he could bench press a lot, maybe three or four plates on each side. But now black marks dot his pecs, little blood trails coming down from them.

"Are those—"

Shaw grunts. "Cigarette burns. Yeah."

The man's arms hang down from his shoulders in a way Jack doesn't like. When Shaw starts to move one, he looks away, down at the ground to the guy's black loafers. If you gave him a push, he would swing from the pipe.

"Shit," Shaw says. "These are not the Russian motherfuckers you want to upset."

Shaw pulls a knife out from his jacket, opens it, and cuts the straps. The guy falls into a heap on the floor, first leaning down over his feet, then his whole torso flops back and his head hits the wall behind him.

Now Jack can see his face. He's Asian, someone Jack's seen before.

"You know this guy?" Shaw asks.

It falls into place: the other cop, O'Malley's partner. Matsumoto. This is the guy who called Hopkins in for the meeting, who gave Jack the bad look.

Above them is a crash that has to be the front door giving way to the police battering ram. Then more yelling, the sounds of Isaak and the cops going back and forth. Jack can't tell what they're saying.

"Let's go."

Shaw bends down to look at the guy's face, looks back at Jack. "I think this fuck's still alive."

"Are you serious?"

Shaw nods.

"You don't want to take him with us, do you?"

"Shit, no. Those are his boys upstairs. They'll find him. Then he can—"

A noise comes from Matsumoto, and then a bubble of blood forms over his mouth. He coughs and looks up at Shaw, coughs again, spitting a mouthful of blood onto his sternum.

He manages to get out, "Thanks. Thanks for cutting me down."

Then Matsumoto looks up for the first time and sees Jack. He stares Jack down, smiling through the blood on his mouth. "Palms," he says. "You'll fucking die in this shit, just like Hopkins."

As fast as he's said this, Shaw squats next to him and pulls the guy's head back by his hair. It's shaved almost bald on the sides, with spikes on top and long wisps in the back. Shaw's got him by the long stuff.

This is when Jack starts to hear heavy footsteps pounding through the front rooms upstairs. It won't be long until they find their way down the hall, figure out the books on the bookcase are fakes and start knocking down the door.

Shaw brings his face right down alongside Matsumoto's and asks, "Who killed Mills?"

Matsumoto laughs, coughs up more blood. "You did. Palms did. Who didn't?"

Shaw pulls down harder on Matsumoto's hair, snaps his head straight up. He chops Matsumoto's neck across the Adam's apple, then lets go of the hair when a fresh coughing fit starts up. As a last insult, Shaw slaps the back of Matsumoto's head, knocking it forward, and Matsumoto promptly spits up more blood into his lap.

"You killed him, you fuck." Shaw stands, dusts off his hands.

Shaw makes like a model on *The Price Is Right* and offers up Matsumoto like a prize. "You want to kick this fuck?" he asks Jack.

"No." Jack nods toward the hole where the girls left. "I think we should keep moving."

"Right," Shaw says. He swings his right hand like a golfer and connects with a hard slap across Matsumoto's forehead, sending Matsumoto's head flying back into the wall. He follows this by stomping down on Matsumoto's ankle, crushing it against the floor. This elicits a loud scream from the crooked cop, which brings a shuffling of feet and stomping upstairs.

Jack starts to head toward the hole and sees a big sheet of linoleum on the floor in front of it. "Let's go," he whispers to Shaw.

Shaw bends down, jabs his finger in Matsumoto's face. "Never, ever sell out a good cop. You hear that?" He grinds down harder on the ankle but clamps his hand over Matsumoto's mouth this time. "Do you hear me?" He nods Matsumoto's head for him, hitting it against the wall as he does.

Jack hears footfalls pounding down the hall.

"Good," Shaw says, whacking the mullet against the wall one last time and stepping away. He wipes his bloody hand on Matsumoto's shirt sleeve, says, "You better hope I don't see you again."

47

Through the hole in the wall, Jack sees the girls waiting for him, no longer crying. They wave anxiously at Jack when they see him. They're standing in a tunnel with white walls—bricks painted over—a single bare lightbulb hanging above them. From its direction, Jack guesses the tunnel leads back underneath the street. Wherever it goes, it's a way out. For now.

"Let's get this," Shaw says, lifting one end of the linoleum. Jack steps a leg through the hole and takes the other side. He holds the linoleum in place as Shaw steps into the tunnel, then the two of them position it against the basement wall as Jack comes all the way through. It's definitely not impenetrable, but it might slow someone down for a minute or two—less if Matsumoto tells them where to go. Jack figures it won't be long before he figures out it's the police above him, starts yelling to tell them where he is.

"Come on." Shaw's already starting down the tunnel, the girls right behind, moving like they've been through here before.

At the other end of the tunnel is a step down and an entrance into what looks like another basement. Here the girls wait for Shaw and Jack to lead, to fight their way through the cobwebs that hang along the ceiling and the dusty furniture blocking any clear path through the room. Whoever owns this basement clearly hasn't been down here in a while. How Gray Suit stumbled through, Jack has no idea.

But they move around the old couches, dressers, and a file cabinet. The room doesn't seem to lead anywhere—a set of wooden stairs heading up to the house appears to be the only exit—until the girls lead them to pile of toppled-over cardboard boxes behind the stairs, and beyond these there is another hole, which leads right into another basement.

In this fashion, Jack, Shaw, and the girls make their way through four basements and two tunnels until they come to a basement stocked with food items and the girls head straight for the staircase up. Except for the second basement, the path has been more or less clear, as if Gray Suit had just stumbled through the same route, turning on lights and knocking down any barricades that lay in the way. But here the path ends: this basement, these stairs.

"I guess this is the place," Shaw says.

Jack's been trying to follow their movements in his mind, to connect them to his idea of the street above. "The café?" he asks.

They watch the girls go up and then stop at the top steps. "You come?" the blond says. "You come."

The other girls look concerned, like they want to make sure they're not alone in the world without Jack and Shaw.

"Yeah," Shaw says, drawing his gun. "Okay."

The girls stand to one side and let Jack go first. He climbs the stairs, listens at the door. From the other side, Jack hears low talking: a woman's voice and a man's. He left the Kalashnikov under a couch in the second basement because of its size, but he still has the revolver he got off one of the guys in the café. Now he removes the gun from the back of his pants, holds it next to his head.

"Go on," Shaw says. "Open it and let's get out of here. This dust is fucking with my allergies."

Jack turns the handle slowly, trying to keep the door quiet. The latch releases, and he opens the door enough to see tall stacks of boxes: cases of coffee and sugar. He can hear the voices more clearly now. The woman has an accent and her voice sounds familiar, the man's voice authoritative. But he still can't make out what they're saying.

"All right already!" Shaw pushes through Jack and out into the room beyond the stairs. It's a storage space, a pantry filled with everything you'd need to run a café. Shaw steps out of the small room through an open door frame, and Jack follows. They walk out behind the counter of Tedeschi's Café.

Standing in the café, looking at them in disbelief, are the girl who rang them up for a crème brûlée not an hour before and Black Suit. As far as Jack can tell, he's wearing the same suit that he was back in the alley. They both raise their hands when they see Shaw's gun pointed at them. The girl has fresh blood on her chest, possibly her husband's.

"Well, fuck me," Jack says. "Seems we've run into each other again." He comes around the counter and feigns a punch at the Russian's crotch. The guy winces and starts to double over even before Jack pulls back.

Shaw looks around the café. The dead men are in the same positions inside the room. The woman's husband is gone from the sidewalk outside. "Your man get some medical treatment?" he asks.

She nods, her hands still raised by her head.

"That's good," Jack says. "He needed it." He backs away from Black Suit toward the woman, and then turns fast, blindsides the Suit with a big, sweeping right cross. The Russian goes down hard on the floor. "That's for the alley."

Shaw walks across the room toward the door. "That BMW out there," he asks. "Is that yours?"

Black Suit nods as Jack stands over him.

Jack reaches inside the guy's jacket and finds the keys. He thanks the guy.

"Were the cops here?" Shaw asks.

The woman nods.

"But it's too soon for them to be gone," Shaw says. "They were barely here."

Black Suit shakes his head. He says in a rough voice, "We take care of our own people. We do not need police."

"Is that so?" Shaw says. "Well, then, we can be going. Let's go, Jack."

Jack steps away from the Suit toward the door. This is when the three girls from the house step into the room.

The woman lowers her hands to her face, says something in Russian. "Svedka," she says, approaching the blond. The pale girl pulls herself away from the woman, steps toward Jack and Shaw. The other girls follow, backing their way to the front door of the café.

Jack goes to the door, more interested in getting out of North Beach without a police escort than with any Russian reunions.

As Black Suit sits up, he opens his mouth in a wide smile, and Jack sees the same crooked teeth he'd seen a few nights before, the same rows of tombstones.

"You two are *fucked*," he says. "You take Alexi's girls from his house?" He shakes his head. "When he comes back, he will *kill* you."

"Where's Alexi?" Shaw asks.

Black Suit laughs. "He is coming here tonight, right now." He starts to reach into his jacket. "Here," he says. "Let me call and you can speak to him. Make appointment."

Shaw drops his gun right in front of the guy's face, the barrel not eight inches away from the crooked teeth. "Let me guess. You're André?"

Black Suit nods. He hasn't moved his hand since Shaw put the gun in his face.

"Oh, you don't want to shoot André," Jack says. "He's *André*."

"Nah. He's not worth that." Shaw pushes André's hand out of his jacket with the barrel of the gun, then stands up straight. He switches his gun to his left hand and throws a punch right in the middle of André's face. It's a quick punch, and it knocks the guy flat. Jack hears his head hit the tile floor with a crack.

For a full five seconds, the time it takes the girls to cross the room to the door, André lies stunned, not moving.

Opening the door to let the girls out, Jack sees a black BMW M6 idling where Shaw must have seen it before and points the girls toward the car.

André raises just his head—blood trickles down around his mouth—and smiles again, showing his bad teeth. "You should have paid attention to your burned bed, Jack Palms. You two will be dead before morning."

"Anyway," Shaw says. "Thanks for letting us borrow your car."

Jack holds the door open for Shaw. "I drive," he says.

48

Jack drives the BMW out of North Beach fast, going toward the waterfront and Fisherman's Wharf, and then bears right toward the Embarcadero from the other side of Telegraph Hill. The girls in the backseat speak fast and quiet in Russian.

"You believe that shit about the parrots?" Shaw says as they're driving below Coit Tower.

"Yeah," Jack says. "Yeah, I do. Call Gannon."

Jack gives the M6 more gas and feels the muscle of the engine. This is a new-model car he can trust. The thing has a V10, 500-horsepower engine, even nastier than his old Mustang, and Jack feels a little guilty about his pleasure, as though he's cheating on his wife with a younger woman. Still, when they get to the Embarcadero, he's looking forward to opening it up.

He knows Shaw understands that Gannon can smooth over the police situation on Prescott, that she'll have to be the one to go back and shut the house down.

Jack glances sideways at Shaw, sees the officer hasn't made a move for his phone.

Finally Shaw grunts. "Yeah," he says. "I'll call her."

Even with the M6 engine revving into the red as they pick up speed on the Embarcadero, Jack can hear Gannon through the phone. "Yeah, but—" Shaw tries to get a few words in and then hands the phone to Jack. "You deal with this, Palms. It was your idea."

"Jane," he says. "This is Jack."

"So now you probably want me to come help you somewhere? You want me to protect you?"

"No, we have three girls that we're bringing over to get some protection. We took them out of the house."

"Three girls? Bring them here."

It's clear to Jack that Gannon didn't go home and get some rest. He hears a voice in the background on her end.

"Where are you now?" she asks.

"On the Embarcadero. I want you to get someone over to the house on Prescott. The police are there now, and I don't think any of us know what they'll do."

"Shit," she says.

"Yeah."

"Where's Akakievich?"

"We haven't seen him. But I have it on good authority that he's going to be *pissed*. That's why we have to bring these girls in tonight and shut him *down*."

Jack knows that she's not sure whom to trust, that anyone she calls might be closer with Clarence than with her. But he doesn't want to hear about the red tape she'll have to sift through to get the scene under her jurisdiction. He just wants to bring the girls in, get tonight under control, and hear that someone's found Akakievich. For all Jack knows, Akakievich is out dumping the other girls now. Jack's hoping Gannon can get something done for them, wherever they are.

"How many of Akakievich's guys are at Prescott right now?"

"None. They had nothing left. Shaw and I walked in and out of Prescott and our biggest problem was the police."

"Shit," Gannon says.

"That's right. But you can handle it, Jane. You're a federal agent."

In the passenger's seat, Shaw shakes his head. "She's going to be pissed about that one."

Jack can see the Ferry Building ahead of them, knows he's about to pass the turnoff for the Gannons' condo, but he's still enjoying how fast he can take the M6 on the wide street.

On the phone, Gannon's quiet. Then she says, "All right. I'll make some calls. You two come in. No matter what my orders are."

"Call some of your people and get them set up to deal with the situation at Prescott," he says. "But don't tell them where we're heading."

"Yes, sir," Gannon says. "And, Jack?"

"What's up?"

"I just want to say fuck you."

Jack looks at Shaw. "She's happy about this," he says.

"Sure, Jack. Sure she is."

49

Jack eases off the M6's muscle, getting ready to turn around and head back toward Market.

"Shit." Shaw laughs. "I can take my ass home to Walnut Creek right now and get into bed with my wife, fuck her in the morning, do something with my kids. We can even take these ladies back to my house—no one will find them there."

Jack looks into the rearview mirror, sees the sixteen- and seventeen-year-old Russians. "You sure that'll be okay with your wife?"

Shaw takes a look back at the girls. "Hello, ladies," he says. He turns to Jack. "Yeah, fuck that. Let's go to Gannon's."

Jack hits the brakes and makes a hard U-turn across the whole Embarcadero at an empty intersection. At this hour, he practically has the road to himself. "I thought you'd see it that way."

They both laugh as the M6 picks up speed, heading back toward the financial district and Gannon's condo. Her husband will probably still be up with her, though it's likely he's not going to be happy about five late-night visitors. But he's an agent; he knows how it goes.

"What I don't understand," Jack says, "is why Akakievich

goes all out after the squeeze. He's already got himself connected, protection, the club drugs, the girls. Why's he want more?"

"Motherfucker knows that shit won't last. Whoever told him the Feds came in, he knows it's all going to get too big to contain pretty soon."

Jack can see Market up ahead, and he starts to slow down. Here there'll be more traffic and perhaps a few cops. The last thing he wants is to get pulled over.

"Let me tell you a story, Jack. You ready?"

Does he want to hear a story from Shaw? Jack's not so sure. "Go ahead."

"Okay. You got this cage of mice, right? The cage is their home. They're all the same kind of mice. White ones, gray ones. All the same.

"Then there's this piece of cheese in the cage for the mice to feed on. Enough to go around. All the mice can eat whenever they want. And they're happy as shit. No worries in mouse land."

"Okay."

"But then one mouse decides he's getting a little bored with happy. He wants something else. So he bites the mouse next to him on the ass. Then he goes back to eating cheese. You know what? Now that mouse is even happier. He's smiling and laughing his ass off all the way to the cheese wedge. All the other mice want to know how he got so happy. They're jealous.

"And you know what else? That mouse that got bit on the ass, he's *pissed* off. He's like, 'What the fuck!' So he goes and bites another mouse on the ass. Now that guy's pissed, but mouse two is happy again. He's laughing because now he knows how good it feels to bite one of the other mice in the ass."

Shaw pauses for a few moments, looks back at the girls in the backseat. They're looking at him, but they probably can't understand what he's saying.

"So?"

"Now you got happy mice, angry mice, and jealous mice. Next thing you know, you got all the mice in the cage eating cheese *and* biting each other on the ass. They're not necessarily happier in the long run, but once this ass-biting gets started, there's no going back. It's just a part of their lives. And they all start eating less cheese. You see what I mean?"

"You're saying you want to bite my ass?"

"This world, San Francisco, wherever you go, we are those mice. That's us. This our cage."

Jack turns off the Embarcadero, brakes at a light in the first block and says, "I say we make it to Gannon's, get these girls to some kind of safety, then go back to Prescott."

"That's fucking crazy. Think no one will identify us as the dudes who just shot up the whole street?"

"Because it's crazy is why I like it. Who cares if they can identify us? If we go in with a carload of Feds, what can they say? Then we go after Akakievich."

"Yeah. That there, you *definitely* don't know what you're talking about. This dude's up against the city, ready to take on that kind of heat, and you just want to hit him?"

"Only way to take out a bully. You have to hit him first."

Jack jumps the M6 around a turn, revving the engine between gears. "We fucking hit his ass, pound that Russian fucker."

Shaw starts to laugh. "You're nuts, Palms. Fucked in the

head. You sure you're not still shooting H?"

Shaw's still shaking his head as Jack pulls up to the entrance of Gannon's garage. He parks next to the call box, but the doors have already started to open. "Jane must've been waiting for us," Shaw says.

Inside the garage, signs everywhere say the first level is reserved for residents and visitor spots are downstairs. Jack thinks about taking an empty resident space but doesn't see any. Besides, someone calling security to have a stolen M6 taken out of his or her spot is about the last thing he and Shaw need. And why wouldn't they want to hang on to this car? He heads down below, to the second level.

"So we go with the Feds," Shaw says. "But the way I see it—"

Before Shaw can finish his thought, the window beside Jack crashes inward, spewing glass all over the front seats, covering him. At the same time, the dashboard in front of Shaw explodes; paper bits from the glove compartment and an airbag blast out at him.

And the girls in the back start screaming.

50

"Fuck!" Jack slams the gas and tears across the lower level of the garage, heading for the back.

"The fuck!" Shaw paws at the limp airbag, pushing it off his lap, trying to free his arms. It has a hole in it, and the smell of stale aerosol fills the car. "Everybody all right?"

The girls haven't stopped screaming. They sound like a three-part chorus. Each of them screams until she has to draw a breath, but in this way they overlap and it never stops.

Jack hits the brakes and then the gas. He checks the rearview mirror for an instant and doesn't see the girls. He doesn't see any blood either. Jack's driver's-side window is shattered, gone. The BMW's tires screech as he brakes around a turn at the end of a row, then it skids and crashes into a concrete wall.

"Seat belts!" Sparks fly off the door as he accelerates into the open aisle that runs along the back of the garage. He scrapes the M6 along the wall and then veers away, the side mirror completely gone.

Another loud shot echoes out: the same boom he heard when Hopkins was gunned down. The car fishtails, and its back hits the wall again with another flurry of sparks before Jack can steer it right. The car bucks as Jack floors the gas pedal.

"The girls there," Shaw says, "no blood I can see."

As they drive the short distance to the other end of the garage, Jack hears two more shots—a shattering of glass in a parked car marks the first, followed by that car's alarm starting up, and a loud *chunk* marks the second as something hits the concrete wall right in front of the BMW. Jack slams the brakes and skids the car to a stop in the corner of the garage, just tapping the far wall with the front end.

Shaw's out his door and on the pavement before Jack can move.

Jack unfastens his seat belt and opens his door. "Anybody want to thank me? How about, 'Nice driving, Jack. Way to get us out of this shit storm.' No?"

He drops out on his side, staying crouched behind the car. The Barrett must be at the other end of the garage, the far corner, judging by the placement of the shots. Here's where Jack's glad to have a gun, not worried about whom he'll have to shoot or what that'll do to him.

"How about nice job stopping like this?"

He can see the girls lying along the backseat of the BMW, crowded against the back of the front seats. They've stopped screaming, but car alarms echo everywhere, electronic screams all around. Jack pushes the front seat forward, and the first girl slides out of the car onto the cement.

Shaw yells, "How about get your fucking head down and let's get to this fuck shooting a heavy artillery cannon?"

Jack drops into a sitting position, his back supported by the car's rear panel. "Yeah," Jack says. "I guess that'll work." He checks the bullets in the cylinder of his gun, the little revolver he's had since the café. Shaw's got the rest of the bullets, so Jack's glad to see it's still full.

Shaw says, "Girls, stay the fuck down."

The other two girls are out of the car; all three of them in a low crouch along the car's side panel, too much bare leg against the hard, scratchy concrete. Jack wishes he'd found them a blanket or something.

"Stay here," he says. And then to Shaw, "So what's the plan? You want to rush him or flank him?" Jack waits but doesn't hear any response.

"Shaw?" He ducks to the pavement and looks under the car, but the cop's already gone.

51

"Okay."

Jack looks around the garage. From where he is behind the BMW, he can see two walls and the dark concrete ceiling, the pipes and sprinkler system that run along it. Beneath the car he can see the tires of another car parked in a nearby row, but no Shaw, nobody.

Chunk: a shot blasts into the wall above the BMW, raining down pieces of concrete and dust onto Jack and the girls. The report of the gun echoes across the garage. "Yeah," Jack says. "I hear you."

The girls huddle together, crying quietly now. Jack reaches out to touch the blond's leg, her knee. She's shaking, her skin cold with goose bumps.

"I'm sorry," Jack says. "But I'll be back. We'll get help for you."

He drops to the floor and starts a low crawl around the back end of the BMW toward the closest row of cars, just as another shot pummels the concrete wall and a new series of car alarms starts ringing.

"Shit." He ducks his head for a moment and hears another shot crash through the air above him. Chunks of white wall spray across the trunk.

He starts the crawl again and gets to the first car in the row, a Land Cruiser SUV, one of the newer ones, a car some SF guy will probably make sure never sees dirt. Jack sits up on his haunches, wondering about the best plan of attack and where Shaw's gone. The thing to do is probably run the length of the rows, try to get to the opposite corner of the garage without being spotted. Making it that far at a crawl or a crouch will hurt, and if he gets there, it'll mean the sniper has a shot at him, but that's also what it'll take to get a shot at the sniper.

Jack considers Shaw's two-finger motion outside the house on Prescott Court. *Commando time.*

"*Jack.*" Shaw's voice comes from the other side of the row of cars in a magnified whisper.

"Yo."

"Come around this way. I want to show you something."

Jack looks around the end of the SUV and sees Shaw crouched behind the car it faces. He makes the low crawl with his tail in the air and gets to Shaw as another blast from the gun cuts into the wall near the BMW. The girls scream.

Shaw hits Jack on the shoulder when he's close enough, and Jack sits down, his back against the car's rear bumper. "What's the plan?"

"Look," Shaw says. Jack follows his finger to see an extra piece of metal along the pipes and sprinklers on the far roof of the garage. "That's the gun."

Jack tries to look closer. What he sees is a small piece of pipe, what looks like a regular ceiling pipe but thinner, with a short horizontal piece stuck onto its end.

"*That's* the gun?"

"Yeah."

"Is Gannon shooting at us?"

Shaw shakes his head. "I tried calling her to see if I could hear the phone. I didn't."

"She answer?"

Shaw nods.

"So who's—"

"I'm just hoping he's alone, but don't count on it. If he stays there, we're okay. He starts to move, whole new game."

"Let's go get that fucker."

"Right." Shaw points toward one wall, then the other. "I go this way." He points down the row toward the elevators. "And you go there." He points down along the ends of the rows, along the wall parallel to the elevators.

"We shoot when we see someone?"

Shaw nods. "Yeah. That works."

The two exchange a fist pound.

"You sure you ready to shoot that thing?" Shaw nods at the gun. "I don't want either of us getting hurt from hesitation."

Jack nods. "I'm ready."

52

Shaw takes off toward the elevators, crawling along the cars'
bumpers. He's better at crawling than Jack—probably had some
experience in the military, where they teach crawling as a basic
survival skill—and Jack watches him go for a moment before
realizing he'll never be able to copy what Shaw does. Wherever
Shaw's used this shit before, Jack doesn't even want to know. It's
more like Jack to run in, go flat out, and hope the sniper can't
keep up with him or hit a moving target.

He thinks back to the morning with Hopkins, though, and
to what O'Malley looked like in the photos he saw, and he knows
he doesn't want to end up like that.

Jack stays down the best he can. How many people they're
going after, who they are, these are questions that rush through
Jack's head, things he wants—but isn't dying—to know. Then
he hears footsteps, an echo in the garage, and sees movement at
the end of the aisle. Someone who isn't Shaw is moving across
the garage, and Jack dives into one of the rows. He's lucky he
was at a point between cars, had a space to duck into.

Staying low, Jack moves forward across the open driving
space between the rows to a space between two cars on the other
side. Now, instead of moving along the wall, he moves between

parked cars, listening for movement.

He hears a single footstep ahead and something dropping to the floor. On all fours, Jack edges forward like he saw Shaw do.

From down in this position, he's able to lower himself enough to take a look under the cars; he checks for feet or legs in the direction of the wall. Nothing. And then, about two cars away from Jack, a pair of legs and men's black shoes. Jack ducks and waits, hoping not to be heard. The shoes turn toward the elevators. Jack can see their sides, and then they get narrower as they turn to face him again.

Slowly he slides himself underneath a parked car. It's a Volvo—why this car can't be a big Land Cruiser with higher ground clearance, he doesn't know—but he gets under by moving sideways on his hands and his toes. He hears the footsteps coming closer, heading toward the near wall. Just as he hears them pass his row and start away, Jack puts his head close to the car's side and sneaks a look out into the row. He can't see the man at first, but then he passes along the end of the row, his head turned the other way, obscured by a black ski mask. Wonderful. Jack pulls his head back fast because of what else he saw in that moment: The guy was standing straight up, scanning the aisles, and holding a big machine gun like the AK-74 from Prescott.

Jack thinks it over. He knows that a gun that big isn't effective in close quarters, between two tight rows of cars, and that he's best off just going at the guy, getting as close as he can. He's been charging right at his targets so far, not showing any fear, even doing a passable impersonation of Sergeant Mike Haggerty's driving when he pulled into the garage. This is real fucking life, Jack knows, and not a movie, but he's not about to stay tucked under a parked car. That's not acting *or* action.

He slides his body out into the gap between the cars and gets into a push-up position. He hears the footsteps on the far side of the next row.

"Yeah," Jack says under his breath, trying to fortify himself. This is the time, as he sees it, and there's nothing to do but act on what's here.

This is life.

53

Jack gets ready to raise himself for a look around. He moves up only enough to see through the back side windows. All he sees is more cars, the rows between him and the guy with the gun.

"Yeah," Jack says. He's starting to nod, getting into it now, his blood and adrenaline pumping. *Do or die* time, maybe *do or do*, he hopes. He's not Mike Haggerty, but Jack Palms is ready for the task.

He makes a fast crawl to the end of the car and then cuts right toward the direction he saw the guy moving. The two cars he slides between are parked tighter, and he has to stand partially to get between them. He keeps his head down, expecting to hear the loud boom of the Barrett.

The windows of an adjacent car shatter in the spray of an automatic weapon, and Jack squeezes himself onto the ground.

"Fuck."

He shakes the glass off his jacket. No sounds of Shaw, no footfalls or anyone calling his name. Nothing.

Jack gets down lower, flat against the cement floor of the garage, and looks under the car.

Not ten feet away from him, he sees the dark shoes—legs standing still, pointed in his direction. Then the AK-74. From a prone position, Jack jumps up onto a hood just in time to avoid a round of shots fired under the cars. He falls off the front of the hood and sees the shooter around the end of the second car in front of him.

With a quick shot from the revolver, Jack makes the shooter duck and runs around the car, closing ground.

As the shooter starts to stand again, Jack clambers onto the hood of the closest car and lunges at him. He hits the masked guy at his chest before he can raise the AK, and they both tumble back into the open space of the aisle.

Mask rolls and Jack lands on his shoulder, the hard bone hitting concrete and sending a shockwave through Jack's arm. He knows it's what has to be done; and if he's alive to feel his shoulder tomorrow morning, it's a great fucking world.

Jack switches the gun to his left hand as he comes up and then blocks himself into Mask again as the guy squeezes off a few shots that cut up a nearby car and ricochet off the ceiling as he loses his balance. Jack doesn't stop, though; he keeps his legs pumping and driving through the guy's body, knocking him back and horizontal over the garage floor so he has to use his hands to catch himself. Fuck if Jack's going to let him keep his hands on that machine gun.

Mask rolls, and Jack jumps onto his back, driving him into the floor before he can get up. This second tackle knocks the guy flat and away from his gun. But as Jack tries his best to hold him down, Mask fumbles for something else along his belt, and Jack feels too much movement underneath him. Chances are he won't be able to hold on long. Where's Shaw? And who is this guy he's fighting?

As Jack concentrates on Mask, the guy throws his head back, a move Jack's got to learn to see coming, and catches Jack right in the nose—hard enough for him to see stars. Jack squeezes his eyes shut and open, trying to clear his vision against the tears. He takes an elbow to the head and a shot to the ribs as Mask rolls him off with a turn and a hard knee, and Jack winds up between the guy and the AK.

This is the luckiest thing to happen to Jack all week. He almost falls over the gun as he rolls backward—his eyes still teary from the pain in his nose—and before he knows it, the guy's on top of him, punching him just as Jack gets his arm up to cover his face. The punch deflects off Jack's forearm and hits him in the nose.

The good part about getting hit in the nose…there's no good part about getting hit in the nose.

Jack's eyes water and he loses sight of the guy again as he brings his gun up. Mask grabs onto the revolver, and the two wrestle over it, rolling over each other. Jack fights to hang onto the gun with both hands, gradually getting past the teary eyes to see Mask again.

He's on his ass with Mask on top of him when he does.

Mask fires a left hook at Jack's ribs, but he isn't able to get enough on the punch to do any real damage. Jack tangles his legs with Mask's, trying to hold him and hit him with the gun. They roll again and, in a moment of balance, Jack gets on top and shoves his forearm into Mask's neck. He knocks the back of Mask's head against the concrete once, hard, and feels the other's grip loosen on his gun. Jack hits the guy's head on the ground again, harder this time.

But then the hands on Jack's are strong again, and they hold him steady as the guy knees Jack in the thigh with a strong leg from underneath. As the pain washes in, Jack remembers how much a charley horse can sting.

Oh, the lessons he's learning.

Mask pulls the gun from Jack, and he can feel pressure on his finger in the trigger. Jack pushes the gun up, away from his body, but Mask keeps pointing it toward him. Then the gun goes off.

The gun's right by Jack's ear, and he winces from the sound, his eyes stinging from the flash.

Then Shaw's there, his Beretta pressed up against the side of Mask's head. With one foot, Shaw pushes Mask's shoulder flat so he rolls off Jack and onto the cement to look straight up into the barrel of the gun.

"This clear enough for you?" Shaw asks, both hands on the gun and his finger on the trigger. He spreads his legs to push the gun toward Mask's face.

Jack feels a growing warmth in his shoulder and knows something has gone terribly wrong.

"Okay," Mask says in a voice Jack's heard recently enough to recognize.

54

"Take this fuck's mask off."

Jack sits up. He looks at Shaw and then back at the guy. It takes him a few moments to steady himself, but he does. "I think I might be shot," he says.

Shaw looks over at Jack, then goes for the mask, pulling it up over Tom Gannon's chin to reveal his face.

Tom's breathing hard.

Jack wipes his mouth with the back of his hand, sees the streak of blood it leaves along his wrist.

"A crooked Fed?" Shaw bends down at the knees and touches Tom's face with the barrel of his gun. "You kill some cops with that cannon? You do my friend Mills?"

"Freeze. All of you." The voice is female—and angry.

On the other side of the aisle, Jane Gannon comes forward holding a snub nosed service revolver, aiming it directly at Shaw. "What the fuck are you two doing?"

Shaw looks at the Gannons: first at Jane, then at Tom, and then back at Jane.

Jack slumps backward onto his butt, holding his good arm up by his head. He can feel his nose bleeding and taste the blood in his mouth. The pain from his shoulder starts to roll in now and it's bad—an extra-large helping of hurt. It's like a big thug just punched him in his shoulder muscle and gave him a charley horse as big as his thigh.

Still, having a gun pointed at him has a way of making everything seem crystal clear, as if a new light has come on in the garage and slowed the world.

Shaw stands and backs away from Tom, still aiming his gun at Jane's husband.

"I'm shot," Jack says.

Jane shakes her head. "What is happening here?"

"Your husband was shooting at us with a Barrett." Shaw looks at her, waits to see how this will register on her face. "He killed Mills."

She squints and wipes her hand over her face. "What are you talking about?"

"Don't listen to him, Jane."

Jack wonders whether she took some time to get it together or kept on drinking after he left her. He knows she's supposed to be ready at all times. He realizes that this—pulling a gun on them—means she's ready.

Jack keeps his hand up. "This is your guy," he says. "The one on the inside with Alexi. The one who killed O'Malley. He heard you set the meet when O'Malley called." "This is Tom, the father of my child." She looks at Shaw again and points the gun at him more aggressively, shaking it at his chest. "Lower your fucking gun and stand down, Officer. Now! That is an order."

Shaw doesn't take his eyes off Tom or move his gun. "Full respect, Jane. But I can't move this gun."

Tom laughs. "Just shoot this asshole, Jane. He's trying to

blame me for shooting Hopkins. I came down here to help these guys and look what they did to me! They're obviously crazy."

Shaw says, "Jane, I apologize, but Jack is right."

"*Lower your weapon,* Officer."

"Look in that corner of the garage," Shaw says, pointing. "Or look at the holes in the BMW over there."

Jack squints to focus in on Gannon. "Jane, just take one look."

Her eyes narrow as she regards Jack. "And I'm supposed to look back so you two can blindside me? That's a good one, but it doesn't work outside of the movies." She shakes her head. "Fuck you."

"Or look at this mask he was wearing." Jack lets his head fall back against a parked car. "I think I need an ambulance, guys."

Shaw turns to point his gun at Jane and steps away from Tom, who starts to gather himself to stand. Tom and Jack both see the AK on the ground at the same moment. It's closer to Jack, about a yard from his feet.

Jack shakes his head. "Don't do that, Tom."

"Look," Shaw says. He and Jane are in a standoff, less than ten feet apart. "We both lower our guns, you turn and look behind you. You'll see a Barrett M107 mounted in the far corner of the garage, by the ceiling. You ask yourself how that got there and who shot it at our car. Ask yourself what that means."

She doesn't turn or lower her weapon; instead she sets her feet apart and squints one eye like she's getting ready to shoot Shaw.

"It's set up on the ramp," he says, his voice still calm. "Ask yourself why your man's got that, why that's here."

She opens both eyes again, doesn't lower her gun.

Jack mouths words that come out as "I'm fucking shot here."

Shaw rotates his gun in his hand, pointing the barrel straight up and removing his finger from the trigger, the weight of the gun resting against his palm, his trigger finger against the guard; he's in no position to shoot. "I'm trusting you, Jane. Now you trust me."

Tom looks at Shaw and then again at the 74. With his right hand on his shoulder, Jack pushes himself against the car with his feet, gathering his legs underneath him.

"Don't listen to these idiots," Tom says as he starts to get up. "They're criminals. Look what they did to me. You going to believe them if they tell you I've been sleeping with Akakievich's hookers too?"

"Oh, Tom," she says. And she turns away, lowers the gun. "Fuck. Fuck. *Fuck! Tom.*" She says this last word, his name, as if she's just heard it all, seen through the curtains that have been there for however long in their lives, as if it's all just come together. Her eyebrows knit together as she looks at her husband. "Please. *Tom?* Not that."

"Jane. You can't believe *these* guys."

"You fucking asshole!" She starts to swing the revolver toward her husband. That's when he makes his move for the AK, the move Jack's been anticipating and dreading since they both looked at the gun. But he's ready. Gritting his teeth against the pain, Jack pushes his body off the car and ducks his head. He falls on top of the AK like a suicide soldier saving his trenchmates from a grenade.

Tom Gannon falls on top of Jack, making hard contact with Jack's left shoulder and knocking him into the ground. The muscle screams and Jack can feel the bullet inside him grinding against his bone.

But Tom can't get to the gun because it's underneath Jack.

A shot goes off right beside them. Jane Gannon lowers her gun at her husband. "Tom, get off him."

Tom flops back onto his ass and raises his hands. His shoulders slump, a slight change in his carriage that says everything,

Jack feels as though he's just been dropped off a small building.

55

A drop of blood trickles off Jack's left hand and hits the floor by his side. Jack grips his shoulder tighter with his good hand, trying to restrict his loss of blood, hoping he won't black out.

"What do you want me to do, Tom?" Gannon says.

Tom shrugs and gets to his feet. "Kill them?" he asks. "You can't let me go down for this."

"What?" Shaw says. He's had his gun pointed up; now he brings his finger back to the trigger, aims it at Tom Gannon.

Tom takes a step toward his wife.

Jane shakes her head. "I'd have done anything for you, Tom."

He steps toward her again.

Jack says, "I think I need a hospital here, people."

Shaw glances over at Jack and laughs. "This boy's actually never been shot before. We should get him to a doctor."

Jane looks at Jack and that's when Tom makes his move. He rushes at his wife and grabs her from the side, spins her so her body is between his and Shaw's. They struggle for the gun, his hand over hers, both of them trying to control where it's aimed. Shaw's trying to get a clear shot at Tom—the clear shot there's no way he will get.

Then Jane stomps on Tom's foot with the heel of her boot

and spins away, surrendering the gun in exchange for Shaw's clear shot. In that moment, Shaw fires, clipping Tom's shoulder. Then as Tom continues to raise and point the gun, Shaw shoots him in the chest, knocking him backward against a car.

Jane rushes to him and takes the gun away, feels under his chin for a pulse. A large bubble of blood comes out of Tom's mouth.

"*You* pulled me back from going after the house on Prescott, didn't you? Did you even call Dockery?"

Tom shakes his head. "Of course not. There was no way you were going in there." Tom tries to say something else and more blood bubbles out of his mouth. He closes his eyes. "I got too far in, Jane." She holds him up, props him in her arms. "I had to kill O'Malley. He was going to tell you."

"That girl in the Chevy, then? The second girl was your whore?" She lets him fall back onto the ground and slaps him. Then she stands up, pointing the gun at her husband. "I should just kill you here," she says.

"Do it." Tom coughs and raises his hand to his throat.

Shaw says, "Jane."

Gannon cocks the hammer. Her husband nods.

"No," she says. "I'm not letting you off that easy."

56

As Gannon stands over her husband, a phone inside his jacket starts to ring. He closes his eyes, his breathing coming in wheezes.

Hearing the phone, Jack feels in his right-hand pocket for his own. If no one else will, he'll call his own ambulance.

Shaw still stands in the same position, his gun trained on Tom.

Jack can't find his phone in the right-side pockets of his jacket *or* his jeans. "Fuck," he says, trying to reach his left pockets with his right hand.

Tom's phone rings again, and he smiles. "That's him, you know."

"Who?" But even as Jane says it, they all know who Tom means.

"He'll be calling to find out where he can collect you. He'll want to come and get his girls."

"That's not going to happen," Jane says.

Tom reaches inside his jacket, wincing in pain from the movement. "You want to be the one to tell him?"

"Sure," Shaw says. "Put the fucker on."

Tom smiles, even through his pain. He clicks his tongue

against the back of his front teeth in a scolding manner. "Better be nice, Officer."

Jack finds his own phone in the inside pocket on his jacket's left side. He takes it out and finds the screen smashed. He swears, pushes a button, and sees the screen light up with no reading. If the phone still works, he doesn't need a screen to help him dial three numbers.

Jane steps over to her husband, reaches into his jacket, and gets his phone. She flips it open. "What? Who is this?"

The phone beeps, a Nextel signal, and an accented voice says, "Thomas?"

It's a voice Jack recognizes immediately. It's the asshole from the Coast, the bald guy with the beard and the gun with the laser sight: Alexi Akakievich.

"No. He's not here."

"The other Agent Gannon? Then this means our charade is up, is it?" The phone beeps.

Shaw says, "Fuck this dude."

Jack holds his phone against his ear but doesn't hear anything. His shoulder has started to hurt less, and he wonders if maybe he's going into shock.

"Is that Officer Shaw? From the Walnut Creek police?"

Shaw shakes his head, doesn't speak. They wait for the phone's second chirp and more from the Russian. "You have my girls. These are *my property*. Understand?" Alexi's voice rises in volume and intensity as he speaks. "You have stolen them from me." The phone chirps again. "You have stolen a car from André. He is also upset."

Jack snorts. "Tell him he can have the car back," he says.

Gannon looks at her husband. "Does this fuck know where we live?"

Tom grinds his teeth, nods.

Gannon swears. "Hold on Alexi, honey, douche bag." She holds the phone against her leg. "We've got to get those girls out of here."

"I'm on it," Shaw says. He steps toward Jack, heading in the direction of the BMW and the girls, and takes Jack's phone.

"Ambulance?"

Shaw hands Jack his gun, the Beretta. "I'm on that for you, Jack. Just keep an eye on Tom."

Gannon moves to follow Shaw. "I'm coming too." She heads right past Jack, dropping the phone into his lap. "Deal with this asshole, okay, Jack?"

Jack looks at Tom's phone in his lap and the gun in his right hand. Tom's not in any shape to move, isn't near any guns, and Jack can watch him. "Alexi, my boy. How you doing?"

"Palms?"

"That is me."

"*Palms*. You are fucking dead, Palms. We will kill you by morning."

"Yeah. You might have to hurry, though; I'm already shot and bleeding."

"Yes, Jack Palms, I can see this."

Jack looks around, unsure if Akakievich is bluffing or if he's really here. It's not outside the realm of possibility.

On the other side of the garage, he sees Gannon talking on her phone, hurrying to get the girls away from the car. Shaw's not with her.

"Did you see what I did to Officer Matsumoto? You must have seen in basement."

Jack hears the creaking of the garage door sliding open, a vehicle entering on the upper level: It's loud, something that sounds big.

"You here, Alexi? Is that you?"

At the bank of elevators, Gannon starts waving toward the upper ramp. She's loading the girls into the elevator now, no longer talking on her phone.

All of a sudden, Shaw's standing next to Jack. "Yo," he says. "Cavalry's here. More Feds."

Jack breathes a sigh of relief. He knows he's not in any condition to deal with an angry Russian mobster.

Shaw looks at the phone in Jack's hand. "You still talking to this guy?"

Jack shrugs, hands Shaw the phone.

"Gotta go now, Alexi. You take care." Shaw looks around on the phone and presses a button. It beeps. He tosses the phone to Tom, who's still lying on the ground, wheezing. It bounces off his chest and hits the ground, chirps again.

Shaw gets under Jack's good arm and drapes it across his shoulders, starts to pull Jack up off the ground. "Easy now," he says.

Jack grunts. He can feel the pain again, but the sight of two big black FBI vans coming down the ramp eases it more than a little.

"For better or worse," Shaw says, "these our boys now."

"Think any more of them were working with Tom?"

Shaw shakes his head. He takes the gun off the trunk and holsters it inside his jacket. "Only one way we'll find out."

"Just tell me they called an ambulance."

57

In the back of the ambulance, Shaw rides next to Jack's stretcher on the way to the hospital. He looks down at Jack in a way that suggests he knew Jack would end up like this all along, shaking his head slowly as he sucks his teeth.

"You know," Shaw says, "Mrs. Agent Gannon feels *really* bad about all this."

Jack knows. Gannon apologized at least three times for her husband shooting him before getting together with a gang of Feds who were there to lock things down and take Tom, the girls, and very nearly Jane into custody. When her superior, a guy named Dockery, showed up on the set as if he owned the whole building, Jane was able to talk her way out of hock, but only barely.

Shaw shrugs. "I almost let her ride with you." He looks at his watch. "You know how much I want to get home, right?"

"A lot." Jack hears his voice come out deep and crackling. He has started to have trouble breathing since the paramedics strapped him down. "You want to fuck your wife in the morning, make breakfast."

"*Exactly.* You know me. But that's how it goes."

Jack looks at the cop.

"Besides, what would you do with all of Jane's fine feminine attention right now? All strapped down and wheezy."

"Luckily, I have you instead."

Shaw laughs. "Seriously, Jack. You know it's better for Jane to handle all that negotiating with those Feds. I'm no good at that shit."

Jack tries to nod, but a shot the paramedic gave him has his body numb all over. He can barely feel his feet.

"We can trust Jane. She's solid."

Shaw nods. "About time you got that."

Jack thinks back to the other Feds strapping Tom onto a stretcher and loading him into another ambulance. Jane could have gone with him, but she didn't even consider it. Things get cold real fast when your husband crosses over and starts swinging with foreign pussy for hire.

Jack feels light, floaty.

"Shame," Shaw says. "Beautiful woman like that. Now she'll be heading for divorce. It would be nice to have her hold your hand in here, eh?"

"My ass." Jack pushes out the words. He can see the white ceiling of the ambulance and the bright fluorescent lights.

"Yeah, I wouldn't believe it either."

"No," Jack says. He speaks softly—it's the best he can do now—and Shaw's forced to bend toward him to hear. "My ass. I want you to kiss it."

Shaw sits up again, laughing loudly. He pats Jack on the leg, a part of his body Jack can still feel. "That's nice, Palms. Real nice. I'm glad to see you haven't lost your sense of humor."

Jack's phone starts to ring. They look at each other, and Jack closes his eyes. It's inside his jacket, the jacket he's only half wearing since the paramedics had to get at his shoulder. Somewhere underneath the straps and under his body, the half of the jacket he's not wearing has his phone.

It rings again.

The ambulance bumps over something in the street that rocks Jack's shoulder as though he's on a boat in the open sea. He closes his eyes to fight the nausea.

"Let me get that," Shaw says. "Might even be Gannon, calling to apologize again."

Jack would bet that it's the angry Russian in the black suit, André, calling to get his car back, or even Alexi, ready to tell Jack he'll meet him at the hospital.

Shaw pushes his hand under Jack to go through his jacket pockets.

The phone rings again.

Jack feels Shaw's hand moving under him, pushing against his ribs and forcing his body against the straps. Even through his drugged fuzz, Jack feels as though Shaw's sticking him with an ice pick.

"Just one second," Shaw says. "I think I can feel it."

The phone rings again as Shaw brings it out in his hand. He flips it open in mid-ring. "Jack Palms's line. He's been shot right now, and he can't come to the phone. Can I take a message?"

Jack angles his head toward Shaw, watches the cop's face to see who the call is from. Shaw's face goes from happy to concerned, as if he's trying to understand what the speaker on the other end is saying. He winces, and his eyebrows squeeze together.

"Say that again." Then he nods. "Sure," he says. "Let me give him that information." He holds his hand over the receiver.

"Some guy, says his name's Vlade."

Jack feels sleep coming on but fights it back, holds his eyes open to look at Shaw.

"Dude says he just got back in town and he wants to take you out to start the party?"

Jack watches Shaw's lips as they move. He wants to say something to stop them, to tell Shaw to hang up on the crazy Czech bastard, even if it really is Vlade and not Alexi, but he's starting to feel dizzy. His eyes close against his will and he fights to open them.

"Right," Shaw says into the phone.

Then Jack's eyes close again and he can hear the EMT saying something, touching his face and letting him know that soon he won't be feeling any more pain.

JOIN THE FAMILY

Enjoy this book? You can make a big difference.

Reviews are my most powerful tools when it comes to getting attention for my books. As much as I'd like it, I don't have the financial muscle of a New York publisher. In truth, most New York publishers don't have much financial muscle anymore either.

On the other hand, I have built something much more powerful and effective than that, and it's something those publishers would kill to have.

A committed and loyal bunch of readers: aka The Palms Mommas and the Palms Daddies—My Palms Family.

Visit sethharwood.com/family to join the group. I'll follow up with special, Family-only content, updates on new material, audiobooks, audio updates, and more.

REVIEWS

Reviews are my most powerful tool when it comes to getting attention for my books. As much as I'd like it, I don't have the financial muscle of a New York publisher.

Honest reviews of my books help bring them to the attention of other readers.

If you've enjoyed this book, I would be very grateful if you could spend just five minutes leaving a review (it can be as short as you like) where you bought it.

Thank you so very much.

ALSO BY SETH HARWOOD
Have you read them all?

JACK PALMS CRIME

Now that you've read the prequel to *Jack Wakes* Up, you're ready to read the original, the introduction to Jack Palms and the first place (in fiction) where Junius showed up.

Jack Wakes Up

Washed-up movie star Jack Palms left Hollywood, kicked his drug habit, and played it as straight as anyone could ask for three years. Now the residual checks are drying up and the monastic lifestyle's starting to wear thin. When Jack tries to cash in on his former celebrity by showing some out-of-town high rollers around San Francisco's club scene, he finds himself knee-deep in a Bay Area drug war.

And the thing that scares Jack the most? He's starting to enjoy himself.

It'll take the performance of a lifetime to get him through it alive.

If you're curious about JUNIUS PONDS and want to read his origin story, you'll enjoy:

Young Junius

In 1987, Junius Posey sets out on the cold Cambridge (MA) streets to find his brother's killer in a cluster of low-income housing towers—prime drug-dealing territory. After committing a murder to protect himself and his friend, he finds himself without protection from retribution. Shocked by the violence he's created and determined to see its consequences through to their end, he returns to the towers to complete his original mission.

JESS HARDING, FBI

In Broad Daylight

During the endless days of an Alaskan summer, a fiend slashes his way through the rural community, where everyone knows your name and always distrusts the outsider. FBI agent Jess Harding treks back to Anchorage to hunt down this sadistic killer who's reemerged from a five-year hiatus—a killer who has already slipped from her grasp once before.

As Jess attempts to immerse herself in the area's culture, she finds a strange rural village inhabited by Russian Old Believers hell-bent on protecting their way of life. Soon Jess needs a safehaven from the glare of daylight—a blood-stained message left at the scene of a murder says she's no longer the hunter, but the hunted.

CLARA DONNER, SFPD HOMICIDE

Everyone Pays

Detective Clara Donner worked vice in San Francisco for years alongside the runaways and vulnerable women who walk the night. She thinks she's seen the worst people can do—until she's assigned to investigate a particularly ruthless serial killer.

As the body count rises and a pattern emerges—each victim is known for his brutal abuse of women—Donner follows the killer's trail across the city. In spite of a nagging sense that the world may be better off without these men, that maybe this killer is doing good, she pursues every lead... until she finds a damaged girl with links to both the killer and his prey. Is this new witness the key to unraveling these murders or another victim left in the killer's wake?

ABOUT THE AUTHOR

Photograph by Eric Fernandez

Seth Harwood is the author of the bestsellers *Everyone Pays*, *In Broad Daylight*, and *Jack Wakes Up*, as well as *Young Junius* and *This Is Life*. He received an MFA from the Iowa Writers' Workshop and teaches creative writing for Harvard and Stanford. He lives in Massachusetts with his wife and daughter. Find more online at sethharwood.com and patreon.com/sethharwood

Made in the USA
Columbia, SC
28 September 2021

46324553R00164